MW01064231

Blue Water

Reverse Fairytales

Little Mermaid book 2

J.A.Armitage

The King

The wonderful feeling of the salty water flying past me as Ari drove me through the ocean never got old. I lived for moments like this when it was just the two of us, swimming through the cool water, jumping over the waves, and sunning ourselves on the rocks away from the media, away from my family and most of all away from responsibility.

We weren't dating...at least, not officially. If any of the press asked me about him, I'd remind them that I was still single, but everyone knew about us. We'd been splashed over the cover of every national newspaper for weeks and a couple of international ones too. So, officially we weren't a couple, but it was no secret to anyone that I ran down to the rocks after my lessons every day, pulled my dress over my head and leaped into the ocean in my swimsuit where Ari would meet me.

Ari swam me back to the rocks, cutting our time together short as I had to go to a dress fitting for Hayden and Astrid's wedding. After everything that had happened over the past few months, they realized how much they meant to each other, and Hayden finally popped the question in a much more fitting way than he had done the first time when he was under the spell of the sea witch.

I picked my way across the rocks, following the route I always did and rushed back inside to take a shower and wash all the salt water from my hair. As usual, I'd spent too long in the ocean and was already cutting it fine, when my father apprehended me with a towel.

"I do wish you'd take a towel with you," he wheezed, handing it over to me. "We are forever having to mop up water."

I looked at the floor behind me and conceded he had a point.

"Sorry, Daddy," I kissed his cheek, jumping back as he dissolved into a coughing fit. "Maybe you should go for a lie-down? You're not looking so good."

He waved his arms around as if to dismiss the notion he could possibly be ill. "You are as bad as your mother. Honestly, now that she's not worrying about the water anymore, she's turned all her attention to me."

My lips curled up at the edges. While it was true that my mother was more relaxed and calm than I'd ever known her since the threat that had been following her for her entire life had been eradicated, her relationship with my father had only strengthened. It had been a shock to him that he'd been married to a mermaid without knowing it, but he was a pragmatic sort and took it in his stride. I guess that was part of what made him a good king.

After bidding him goodbye, I took the stairs two at a time to my room where I pulled off my drenched swimsuit and dove into the shower.

Despite the rush of shampooing my hair and trying to wash my body at the same time, I still managed a little dance of joy at how wonderfully my life had turned out. After my lessons on how to be a queen, I spent every afternoon with Ari having a freedom I never thought I'd have. And the best part was that after Hayden and Astrid's wedding, my parents were allowing me to borrow a sailboat from the royal fleet for a month-long vacation with Ari. I also had to take one of the Palace naval officers to sail the boat and watch over me, but for thirty glorious days, Ari and I would be mostly alone. Not only would I be with Ari, I'd be fulfilling my life-long dream of sailing the ocean. Ari wouldn't be able to join me for long on the boat as when his tail dried, it turned into legs. Legs, which thanks to the sea witch's last spell, caused him great agony. But he could sit on the edge of the boat and dangle his tail fin into the water, or swim beside us. Either way, it was going to be great.

I tried pushing back the little voice that popped up frequently, telling me that there was no future for us. I knew it, but I didn't want to acknowledge it. He couldn't live on the land without great personal pain, and I couldn't live underwater. I was a half-mermaid, but unlike my mother, I couldn't breathe underwater without holding the hand of another mermaid or merman. It made things difficult. To compound the problem, Ari and I were magically bonded. It wasn't something that we chose; it was just something that happened. But neither of us could deny it *had* happened. So destiny had us pegged to spend our days together while reality made it easier said than done. At some point, we would have to go our separate ways knowing that being apart would hurt both of us. Whatever we did, there would be pain involved.

"Urrgh!" I jumped out of the shower, pushing the bad thoughts to one side, and dressed at lightning speed. My mother had offered her study to Astrid to use as a fitting room for all the bridesmaid dresses, so I didn't have far to run, and yet, I still managed to be the last one there.

All eyes turned toward me as I dashed through the door, my hair still dripping wet.

"Sorry," I mumbled, looking for a seat next to one of the younger bridesmaids.

"You'll have to go last," grumbled the seamstress who was currently pinning the hem of a young flower girl's dress. The girl in question, a tiny thing of about four or five looked bored to tears as she was asked to slowly twirl so the seamstress could insert the pins. In addition to the flower girl, there were four others, all dressed in pale blue half-made dresses. My mother watched over them all, but she still managed to give me a steely look as I took the seat beside her.

"I'm sorry," I whispered.

"It's fine," Astrid said, hurrying over to me. "I wanted you to be last anyway. That means you can help me with my wedding dress and tell me what you think. It's a little bit crazy."

I looked at the garment bag hanging up on the wall and wondered what she meant by *a little crazy*.

With her bright green and blue hair, she was going to stand out, no matter what she wore.

Just then, the door opened, and my younger brother, Anthony, stuck his head through the door. One of the other bridesmaids threw a cushion at him and yelled that it was girls only. The cushion bounced off his head and fell to the floor. My mother stood up to see what he wanted, but I jumped up ahead of her.

"It looks like I won't be needed for a while; I'll speak to him."

My mother tutted her disapproval. "Okay, but let him know it was awfully rude to butt in here. I told him that we were using this room as a fitting room. He should have known that the girls would be in various states of undress."

I bit back a smirk. That's probably exactly the reason he'd chosen to look in. He was at that awkward stage. Sixteen years old and second in line to the throne. He'd also managed to have a growth spurt over the summer, adding about five inches to his height and was now taller than I was.

"What is it?" I hissed, closing the door behind me.

"I'm sorry. I forgot you were all in there. I was looking for you, actually. Father said you might be down here."

I chose to believe him although his coming to speak to me was unusual. It's not that we didn't get on. We never had a bad word to say about each other; but the truth was, we weren't close. He was two years younger than me, and a rather gangly looking kid now that he'd grown so quickly. It's like he hadn't given his body time to catch up and so was ridiculously thin despite eating like a horse at every meal. And he never quite knew what to say. Up until a few weeks ago, we barely saw each other except in passing in the palace or at mealtimes. I'd usually be out with Ari or, before I met him, with Hayden and Astrid. Anthony generally liked to go to his room to read. He enjoyed his own company, whereas I liked being around people.

"You found me," I said leading him to a little sofa along the corridor. "What is so important that you'd seek me out?"

He shifted a little, looking uncomfortable. "I wasn't sure of one of the things we learned about today, and I was hoping you'd clarify it for me."

My eyes widened. "This is a turn up for the books—you asking me for help with your studies."

He'd asked to join my preparations for becoming a monarch a couple of months ago. Even though he'd never be king, he wanted to know more about our country. My father thought it a splendid idea, and since then, he'd joined me in learning how to rule the kingdom of Trifork.

I wasn't being totally fair with him. I'd been having lessons like these for well over a year, and so it made sense that I knew more than he did, but it was still a surprise that he came to me for help. He got things better than I did. It was instinctive in him, whereas I had to study hard to retain any of the information. He enjoyed the lessons. No, he loved them. I, on the other hand, tolerated them and spent most of them wishing the time away until I could go and see Ari.

"I was wondering how the kingdoms of Trifork and Havfrue work. I mean, we are heirs to the throne of both, but Havfrue isn't technically a kingdom. What happens if our grandfather dies? Will our mother have to move back there?"

I nodded. Technically, what he said was true. Havfrue, the underwater city that my grandfather ruled was not on any map and was not one of the official nine kingdoms like Trifork was. It was barely a kingdom at all. Really, it was only one city, but it did have a ruler who was a king, so it was kind of a kingdom. As the ruler of Havfrue had no interest in any of the other nine kingdoms (apart from his own family in Trifork) I didn't think it really mattered either way. Most people

9

didn't know mermaids and mermen existed, let alone knew of the existence of Havfrue, and that was the way our grandfather liked it. When the media found out about my mother's origins, Havfrue was catapulted into the press for a while, but since then, things had calmed down.

As for us both being heirs to both thrones, I guess that was true too. If my father died, I would become queen of Trifork. If my grandfather died, as his eldest daughter, my mother would technically become queen of Havfrue, but it was tricky as she was also queen of Trifork through marriage.

"I don't know what will happen if our grandfather dies, but I doubt Mother will move back. She is the queen here. Maybe one of her younger sisters will take her place."

Just then, the younger bridesmaids trooped out of my mother's study along with our mother.

"I've got to go," I whispered to Anthony. "I'm the maid of honor, and the seamstress is a right old bag."

Anthony gave me a grin as I headed back to the study.

The dress that had been picked out for me was the same shade of blue as the other bridesmaid dresses, but Astrid had picked out a material that looked like mermaid scales. It was also cut in a mermaid style. I held it up and raised an eyebrow at Astrid who stood there grinning at me mischievously as if she'd done the funniest thing in the world.

"What?" She shrugged, holding up her hands. "I thought it fitting, given that you are half-mermaid and all, I figured you may as well look like one. Besides, it's a nautical themed wedding because of Hayden's family's naval background. You should see my dress."

"Please tell me you aren't dressing up as a squid or something? I don't think I could take it."

"Silly." She pulled a dress from the final garment bag and held it up. It couldn't have been more different from the dress she wore at the fake wedding a couple of months back. It started off white at the top but had an ombre effect where it went through every shade of blue from the palest sky to the depths of the ocean near the hem. I wasn't too sure if I liked it until she put it on. It matched her hair and her quirky personality perfectly.

"I'm going to match it with some white lilies and have my hair up. What do you think?"

I stared at the pair of us in the mirror. Neither one of us looked traditional in our strange wedding outfits. This wouldn't be to my mother's taste at all, and because of that I was kinda glad she'd left when she had. But seeing us there together, we looked out of this world.

"Sensational!" I replied and meant it. It couldn't have been more perfect.

I pulled down the zipper at the back of Astrid's dress to help her out of it, and as I did, the door to the study flew open.

I turned to find Anthony, red-faced and out of breath.

Annoyance at his blatant rudeness overtook me. With my hands on my hips, I barked a warning at him. "Didn't I just tell you twenty minutes ago not to come barging in here while we are dressing? You can't just do that. I'm going to tell father."

"That's why I'm here," he blurted out. "Father has collapsed. An ambulance has been called for, but he's not breathing. One of the members of staff is doing CPR on him."

Responsibilities

I'd only just talked to him an hour or so earlier. He'd looked ill then, but I couldn't quite replace the image of him berating me for getting water on the floor to one of him lying unconscious. Without bothering to change, I rushed out of my mother's study and raced after Anthony.

We found a whole bunch of people crowded around his recumbent form in the palace entrance way. The grand double height oak doors were open, and I could see an ambulance outside. The crowd of various members of the palace staff parted as Anthony and I got there, and the four paramedics lifted my father onto the ambulance.

"What happened? How is he?" I asked my mother when I found her in the crowd. Behind me, I heard Anthony thanking the members of staff for their help and telling them to go back to work.

"He's breathing now, but I don't know what's wrong. He was found unconscious at the bottom of the stairs, but it didn't look like he'd fallen down them. I think he collapsed before he started walking up them. Can you look after the palace while I'm gone? Ask Anthony to help. I've already asked John to do anything you need. He'll be able to help you with the media. This is bound to get out sooner rather than later, and we'll have to put out a statement. I'll call you as soon as I know more."

I nodded my head as she was helped into the back of the ambulance. The doors closed, the blue flashing lights swirled, and the siren blared. At the bottom of the driveway, the main gates opened and already a group of people had shown up to see what was happening.

As the main doors were closed, I turned to speak to Anthony, but he'd already gone, more than likely helping the staff get back to business as usual.

I had never felt more alone in my life. The huge hallway was now empty of people except the two doormen who stood silently behind me, waiting for instruction.

"You can go back outside," I whispered to them, my voice cracking with the simple command.

They both nodded, leaving me completely by myself and unsure of what to do. I was now the highest ranking person in the palace, and yet, I stood there, rigid and filled with fear, not having the first clue what to do next. My mother had mentioned John. John was the king's chief advisor and my father's right-hand man. If anyone would know what to do, it would be him, and it seemed like a good place to start.

I dashed down into the servant's quarters on the lower level, taking the steps two at a time, trying not to trip over the mermaid style dress as I went. Most of the staff lived locally, but some of the higher staff members had their own quarters, John being one of them. He had the nicest suite with his own kitchen, bathroom, bedroom and living area. I hammered on his door, despite it being the middle of the day and therefore unlikely that he would be there. One of the kitchen staff heard me and shouted down the corridor.

"Ma'am, if you are looking for John, he's up in his office."

Of course! He had his own set of rooms upstairs where he and a number of staff beneath him helped run the palace. In my agitated state, I'd completely forgotten.

Getting up the stairs again was much harder than running down. The dress was tight at the bottom making it difficult to run. Why did I have to be in this ridiculous dress just when my father needed me so?

John was exactly where the kitchen hand said he'd be. As I walked into his office, I found him on the phone. With a somber expression, he held one finger up as if to tell me he was nearly done.

"I said the palace has no comment at this time... As soon as we know anything, we will issue a statement... No, good day."

He replaced the receiver then lifted it again to stop any more calls.

"Bloody press! Your father left less than ten minutes ago, and already, I've had more than five phone calls from reporters. I don't know how they find out so quickly."

John had been in my father's employ since before I was born. From the outside, he was the consummate professional, heading the royal household with poise and discretion. To me, he was like a funny uncle. He was the only member of staff that never referred to me as ma'am, and when we were children, he always had a lollypop ready for Anthony and me whenever we saw him.

He also had a mouth like a sailor and wasn't afraid to use it behind closed doors. Not that anyone on the outside would know such a thing.

"I'm so sorry darling. Come here, take a seat."

His office was originally decorated similar to my father's, only much smaller. Dark wood paneling covered the walls, and four leather seats surrounded the heavy wooden desk. At the window, thick purple velvet curtains hung all the way to the floor. John had added a few touches of his own. Colorful abstract artworks filled the walls and complemented the bright cushions and flowering pot plants on his desk. I'd always felt much more at home in John's office than my father's study, which was regal and stuffy. On the desk, was a bowl filled with candy which John lifted up for me.

I shook my head, trying to keep the tears back.

"Is he going to be alright, John?"

John gave me a sad smile. "I don't know, princess, but I've given the hospital my private number so we'll be the first to hear any news."

He used the term princess as a pet name rather than my title. I'd heard him call some of the staff princess too. That's what I liked about him. He treated everyone the same unless you were from outside the palace in which case he was a gentleman of strength and loyalty to the king and a brick wall if you were a journalist.

"I don't know what to do," I admitted. All the months of lessons had completely left my mind and replaced with fear.

John leaned forward in his seat and offered me a comforting hand on my arm. "Nobody expects you to do anything, so please don't worry about that. I'm ignoring the press for now, but I'll draft a press release as soon as we know more. For now, the official line is "no comment." Anthony thinks it would be a good idea to get all the staff together. I've left him to deal with that, but I think it might be a good idea for you to be there when they congregate. You don't have to say anything. I can do the talking, but they will want to see someone in charge. Anthony mentioned the great hall at two o'clock. You might want to change before then."

I looked up at the clock on the wall. It was a quarter to two. It surprised me that Anthony had the forethought to do anything. All I'd managed to do since my parents left was walk around in a daze and whine to John. I took a deep breath and thought everything through. John was right. The staff needed strong leadership now, not a sappy princess in a mermaid dress.

"Thank you for all your help, John." I stood up from the chair. "I'm going to get changed, and I'll meet you in the hall in fifteen minutes. I think I should be the one to speak, but thank you for your offer."

"As you wish," He stood up too and rounded the desk. As he wrapped his arms around me, I felt the first trickle of a tear fall down my cheek.

Ten minutes later, I was dressed in casual trousers and a smart blouse. I probably should have worn something more formal, but I had no idea of the protocol in such situations. Besides, it was better than the bridesmaid dress.

The hall was packed solid as I entered from the back. It looked like Anthony had done a good job of rounding everyone up as most of the staff were there. At the back, I saw Astrid, and beside her, holding her hand, was Hayden. He gave me a small nod as I passed. Astrid must have called him as soon as she heard the news.

A hush descended as I walked through the crowd to the front of the hall. Anthony was already there as was John. John took a step back as I stepped up onto the raised platform where my parents' thrones stood.

As I gazed out over the hundreds of people I saw every day, it occurred to me that this was my first formal speech. Without having time to prepare anything, I had to speak off the top of my head, which was still in shock at what was happening.

I held my hands behind my back in what I hoped was a suitable pose, but really I was clasping my hands together to stop them from shaking. Fear flooded through me, and my heart beat in double-time as I tried to find the right words to say to the expectant crowd.

"Thank you all for coming up here with so little notice. I'm sure some of you will already know why you are here, but for those who don't, I want to assure you that everything is going to be alright. My father, the king, collapsed just under an hour ago and was taken to the hospital."

I heard the collective gasp rise up through the crowd as they took in the news.

"We don't know what happened, and we don't have any news yet from the hospital, but I want you all to know that you will be the first to hear any updates."

Looking out at each of them, knowing that they were looking up to me as a leader made me realize how wholly unprepared I was for this. I'd had so many lessons on how to be a good queen. I could name all the royal families of all the nine kingdoms, I knew how to address people, I knew the economic status of our own kingdom in relation to the others around us, but I didn't know how to stand tall and lead a kingdom. I didn't know how to make it better for these people, and the staff was only the start. There would be the press to deal with. John putting out a press release was one thing, but they would want to see someone from the palace on the television. I couldn't let John do that. I had a whole nation looking up to me, and I didn't know how to handle it at all. What I actually wanted was to go back to bed, or to escape it all out under the waves with Ari. I took a deep breath and continued my speech.

"You are my father's loyal staff members. Without you, we would not be able to run this house, run the kingdom. I am asking one more thing of you today. John here is in charge of any press in relation to my father's condition. Only he should speak to them. If any reporters try to speak to you when you leave the palace, I ask that you tell them "no comment at this time." You can refer them to John if you wish. The last thing we need right now is the kingdom awash with rumors. I also want to thank you all for your help at this distressing time."

I glanced toward John, and he nodded at me almost imperceptibly. I'd done it. My first-ever speech as head of the household. It made me feel sick.

As the staff shuffled out, I was left not knowing what to do with myself. I sat on my mother's throne and watched the last of the staff leave the great hall, shepherded by Anthony and John. Anthony was turning out to be quite the help in the time of need. Soon, there were only three of us left in the hall. Hayden and Astrid ran over to me. I'd kept strong for the last hour, but as Hayden put his arms around me, I dissolved into a flood of tears. He was my rock, he always had been and feeling him strong by my side, it almost felt like everything was going to be ok. He had a knack for knowing how to cheer me up or make me feel better. We had been best friends for so long that we were in complete simpatico with each other. As the tears flowed, I felt another pair of hands join us, and the three of us ended up in a wet messy three-way hug.

"We've decided to postpone the wedding," Astrid said after pulling back from me. Her eyes were glassy with tears too, although she'd barely spent any time in my father's company.

"Not a chance!" Both Hayden and Astrid looked at me with pity in my eyes. It was nice that they cared, but I didn't want them to change their wedding plans. I didn't want anything to change at all.

"We discussed it," Hayden responded. "It's not a big deal. We can put it back a couple of months, there's really no rush."

"Discussed it?" I looked at the pair of them incredulously. "You only got here ten minutes ago, and I was giving my speech for most of that time. You can't decide to put off the biggest day of your lives over this."

A look passed between them. I didn't like it. I could tell that whatever they were about to say was not something I would want to hear.

Hayden took my hand. "We are due to be married in three weeks. What if the king is still ill? What if he..."

And then, I realized what it was they were really trying to tell me.

They were worried his funeral would coincide with their wedding. They thought he was going to die.

Human Again

"What if he dies? The funeral will mess up your plans." I could feel my chest tightening and pain biting at me. It hadn't occurred to me before now that my father might not pull through. He was still relatively young and up until the last couple of weeks, had always been as fit as a fiddle.

"I'm sorry, Erica," Astrid began, but I cut her off.

"He's not going to die. He's just has a bit of flu or something. He'll be dancing at your wedding, just wait and see."

I didn't wait for a response. My heart felt like lead, and there was only one person I needed, one person that was guaranteed to lift my heart. I took off through the double doors to the balcony and raced down the outside stairs to the promenade. None of the guards tried to stop me. They'd all seen me make this journey enough times in the past few weeks.

I'd only left Ari a few hours previously, but it felt like a lifetime ago. The sun was low in the sky, casting a pink glow over the rippling water. I dashed across the rocks, pulled my clothes off and dived head first into the ocean in only my underwear. When I'd first met Ari, I'd not been able to swim, but after weeks of being in the water for hours every day, I'd become quite proficient at it.

I dived down, holding my breath as I searched the depths for Ari.

Ari, I need you. I spoke to him with my mind, the way we always communicated under water. He would only hear me if he was within a certain distance, but I kept on calling him. When my breath ran out, and it felt like my lungs would burst, I resurfaced, taking in great lungfuls of air.

"Ari!" I shouted out loud, my voice barely audible over the noise of the waves. I took another breath and swam in the direction of Havfrue, the merpeople city that my grandfather ruled over. I found it so much easier to swim under the water where it was calm and serene rather than battle the waves on the surface. Without Ari to hold my hand, I couldn't see nearly as well as I would have liked, and the salt water stung my eyes. I also had to keep going up to the surface to breathe which slowed me down.

Havfrue always seemed so close when Ari took me there or when my grandfather picked me up and took me back to his palace, but swimming there by myself without the aid of a fishtail was wearing. My muscles began to ache with the effort of pulling through the water, and what had seemed so easy with someone by my side was now an arduous task. Still, I persevered, for what was the alternative? Looking back, I could see that I was already halfway there, so swimming in either direction would be equally tiring.

Ari, I cried out, feeling utterly wretched and beyond exhausted. *What are you doing so far out by yourself?* Ari took my hand, and at once, the water appeared warmer. My vision cleared and I could finally see well through the salty water.

I wish I could see better in the ocean when I'm by myself, I began then stopped. The pain in my heart had lifted slightly, thanks to Ari's presence, but the feeling of being overwhelmed persisted. Ari held me close to him as my body shook. He didn't need to ask me anything else to know I was upset. It was pretty obvious. He began to swim with me still wrapped in his arms. I closed my eyes as the warm water cascaded over me, and let him take me wherever he wanted to go. I didn't care. I only cared that I was with him, the location was irrelevant. As it was, when I opened my eyes I found us in the cave of lights. Dark most of the time, it lit up like the water was filled with fairy lights every time anyone swished it around, thanks to the phosphorescence. Ari and I came here often. Occasionally we'd go to his little room in Havfrue, but there was no privacy there as there was no glass in any of the windows and therefore no blinds or curtains. People constantly swam past his room making it feel like we were on display in a goldfish bowl. All the Havfrue people lived the same way, and it didn't bother Ari in the slightest. But I much preferred it here where I could kiss him without worrying about anyone catching us.

As Ari had pointed out, it was hardly a secret that we kissed, but that didn't mean I wanted half the town watching us. I much preferred it here where I could breathe, thanks to the small holes in the ceiling that in the daytime let in light and let in clean air all of the time. I lay back on the beach and let the beads of water drip off into the pale sand. Ari pulled himself up beside me, and I rested my head on his chest

"What is it? What happened?"

Since the sea witch died, Ari was able to talk to me on land. It was only his tail that was still affected by her magic, so he kept it in the water, swishing it every now and again to fill the cave with light.

"My father fell ill. He's in the hospital. Everyone is looking up to me as though I know what to do, and I don't know what to do at all. My mother is with him, so everyone is looking to me to lead them."

My breathing was so rapid that I feared I might begin to hyperventilate. Ari took my hand in his and squeezed it lightly, calming me a little.

"How is he? What happened to him?"

I looked into his eyes, emerald in the low light, and told him what had happened leaving nothing out except the thoughts of Hayden and Astrid. I couldn't bear to tell him that my father might die. Even saying it out loud made it feel like a possibility, a possibility I wasn't ready to acknowledge.

After I'd finished speaking, I lay back on the sand, his arm under my head. He shifted slightly, turning on his side so he could still look at me as he spoke. He rested his free hand on my belly where I grabbed it and held on like it was an anchor, afraid if I let go he'd somehow disappear.

"Stay here with me tonight. I'll keep you warm." He spoke so softly, and yet, I could still hear the slight reverberation of his voice around the cave.

I was still shivering, but it wasn't from the cold, I never felt the cold when I was with him. I was shivering out of fear, out of sadness.

"I can't. I need to be at the palace when my mother calls. I probably shouldn't have come out here, but I needed you."

He pulled me toward him, smothering me in a hug so tight it almost pulled my breaking heart back together.

"If you must go back, I'll take you, but I'm coming too," he replied calmly. "There is no way I'm leaving you alone tonight."

I shook my head sadly. "You know you can't do that." I wanted him to. Oh, how I wanted him to spend the night with me, but we both knew that going on land caused him such agony akin to walking on knives. I couldn't let him do that for me. "Your pain isn't a swap for my pain."

Ari pulled me up so that I was sitting facing him. His tail was still in the water, but I'd pulled my legs up so that just the edge tickled my toes.

"I'm not swapping anything. I hate that we can't be together all the time. Most days, I try not to think about it and enjoy the limited time I have with you. But I can't do that knowing that you need me. I can't change the way things are, but there is no way I'm going to swim around here knowing that you are suffering by yourself in the palace."

"I won't be alone," I shrugged. "Anthony is there. John is there. I have people around me."

"People that will kiss away your tears?" he leaned forward and kissed my cheek. When he pulled back, his lips were wet. I'd not even noticed I'd been crying. He moved forward again and kissed the other side before kissing me on the lips. I don't know if the salty taste of his lips upon mine was from the sea water or from my own tears.

"I'm coming," he insisted.

I closed my eyes and nodded my head. Whatever happened, it would be easier to handle with Ari by my side. He pulled me into the water, and we swam side by side to the shore.

When we surfaced, the sun had gone down entirely, and the only light was coming through the windows of the palace. Not even the moon was shining tonight, and it was too cloudy to see the stars. The clothes I'd left behind were way too small for him, so when his tail dried and turned into legs, he had to hobble across the rocks naked. I thought because of the lack of light we might manage to make into the palace unseen, but I'd not factored in my father's illness. There were a hundred or more photographers at the gate that separated the public promenade from our private one, and every single one of them got a shot of us running into the palace, me soaking wet and Ari with not a stitch of clothes on. What a way to end my day in charge of the whole kingdom.

The palace seemed to be running as it always did. The guards stood sentry, the maids cleaned. A member of staff handed us both a towel. I wrapped mine around my hair; Ari wrapped his around his waist.

"Has my mother phoned?" I asked the young servant I recognized as being one of the office staff under John.

He bowed. "Not yet, ma'am. Do you require a guest suite to be made up?"

He looked Ari up and down as he spoke. I glanced over too, wondering how it might look to everyone. He was a striking man, well over six feet with straight black hair that fell almost to his waist. His chest and arms were pure muscle, but below the line of the towel, his legs were a mess. They looked so much worse than they had the last time I saw them.

The servant raised his eyebrows, waiting for me to answer his question.

Another quick glance at Ari and I knew my answer. "No, thank you. He'll be sleeping with me."

The servant quickly hid his shock, but it was too late. I'd seen the expression on his face. It was the same expression everyone in the kingdom was going to have when they read tomorrow's headlines and saw the photo of us getting out of the water. I wasn't trying to shock anyone. I just really didn't care anymore what everyone thought. I'd already failed at being a good princess enough today. What was an added scandal on top of everything else?

"Can you ask Lucy to bring up some of her cream for Ari's legs and some heavy duty sleeping pills? She can bring them straight to my room. I'm retiring for the evening."

"Ma'am." He nodded his head and turned toward the palace infirmary where Lucy the nurse would be working.

"This way." I ushered Ari to the grand staircase, making note of how unsteady he was on his feet.

"I don't need Lucy's sleeping pills," he said, gripping the banister so hard, his knuckles were white. "I'm no use to you asleep."

"And you are in agony. Don't try to pretend you aren't. Look at your legs."

He looked down. The skin was peeling off all over and deep red lesions covered both legs. It was so bad that small spots of blood were dripping onto the floor where he walked.

"It hurts a little, but I'm here for you."

He put a finger under my chin and slowly brought my face up so I was face to face with him. As I was standing on the step above his, we were almost exactly the same height. He was so beautiful. His green eyes flashed purple for a ghost of a second, telling me his emotional state was high. It was hypnotic how he had a hold of me despite the fact that our only contact was the tip of his forefinger on my chin.

"This is it, Erica. Us, you and me. We are bonded, and nothing can change that. My heart only beats properly when you are near me. The rest of the time it's frantic, wondering where its mate is, skipping beats, and working double-time. It's only when you are near me that I feel completely calm. I don't need the creams and the pills because you are the only balm I need. You are the one that soothes me. No cream can do for me what your presence does, and I think that I am the same for you. I came here to heal your pain, not to have you help me with mine."

It was so true. Nothing felt right whenever he was away from me, and yet, when he was close, everything fell into place. It wasn't that I felt less fearful about my father, but with Ari I was able to manage the pain, to breathe easier. Maybe it was the same for him? I leaned forward and kissed him, and for that minute both of our pain went away.

The Bathtub and Magic

I held his hand all the way up the stairs, and despite his protestations of it not hurting too much, he gripped my hand a little too tightly, letting me know it wasn't true.

In the bedroom he flopped down on the bed and pulled the sheet over his body, leaving his legs exposed to the air. I could barely look at them, and I certainly couldn't do it without my own chest constricting. He looked like the victim of a fire. Even if he refused the sleeping pills, I was going to insist on the cream. As the thought struck, there was a knock on the door. I opened it to find the same servant with the pills and the cream.

"Will that be all, ma'am?" I saw his eyes dart to his left to see Ari lying on the bed. Thank goodness, he'd thought to cover himself up. We'd caused enough gossip for one night.

"Please, can you have some food brought up and a phone? I wish to call the hospital."

He nodded his head and departed.

"I'm not taking the pills. I already told you." Ari sat up in the bed then grimaced as his legs scraped on the sheet beneath them. My white sheet was already spotty with blood from the open lacerations on his legs. Bandaging them might work, but it would also make changing back to his tail impossible.

Instead of arguing with him, I set the pills and cream down on my bedside table and lay beside him being careful not to touch his legs at all. Even the slightest pressure could damage them.

"I wish my grandfather hadn't had the sea witch killed," I mused, putting my hand on his chest. I'd have to get up again at some point as I was still in my wet underwear with only a towel to stop the bed from getting wet, but for now, I just needed the warmth only Ari could provide.

He twirled a wet lock of my hair around in his fingers. "If he hadn't, you would be dead and I'd rather this..."—He pointed to his legs—"than not being able to see you at all."

"Is there no one else in Havfrue that can change this magic?" I'd asked the same question a million times, and Ari always gave me the same answer.

"Your grandfather is a powerful man, the most powerful man in the whole kingdom of Havfrue, but he cannot change this spell. He has tried. You must know that I'm not the only one with this problem. Many people loved the sea witch. She was a manipulator, and many people fell for her lies. Your mother did, I did. Your grandfather has been doing everything he can to help those affected, but it seems that many of the people who got something from the sea witch are now disadvantaged in some way. Some, like me, are in pain."

"You know, nothing happened to my mother when the sea witch died, and my mother was the one person she most wanted to hurt. You'd think if anyone would suffer, it would be her."

It was true. I'd been waiting for my mother to develop some kind of pain or discomfort since the sea witch died, but she'd remained as she always had been, except perhaps, a little happier knowing her children could go in the ocean without anything bad happening to them.

"You don't think my father's illness has anything to do with the sea witch's spell do you?" I asked, sitting up. "She wanted something from my mother and never got it. This could be her final act of treachery."

Ari's eyebrows knotted together as he mulled my theory over. "I don't think so. The people affected are directly affected. Some are having their hair fall out, some are having pains in their limbs, or their voices are changing. Everything she left behind is physical and directly related to the person involved. As far as I'm aware, no one has lost family members because of her spells."

I wasn't so sure. How was it possible my mother got away with it when so many others hadn't?

A knock on my door broke me from my thoughts. I jumped out of bed and yelled through the closed door.

"Just a minute!"

After grabbing a clean set of pajamas from my drawers, I ran into my bathroom, peeled my wet underwear off, and pulled my nightwear on.

It was the servant with a couple of beef sandwiches on a silver tray, along with some tomatoes, salt, pepper, and mustard in case we wanted to add to them. Next to the plates, was the phone I asked for.

I thanked him and let him retire for the night.

Passing one of the sandwiches to Ari, I dialed the number for the hospital. Being a member of royalty meant I had a direct line to the head of the hospital, and it was programmed into the phone.

"Yes?" A man with a steely voice answered.

"This is Princess Erica. I'm calling to inquire about His Majesty."

He paused, and then I heard him cough as though he was clearing his throat.

"I'm dreadfully sorry, Your Highness, but I've been requested to ask you a secret question in case it's not really you. The paparazzi have been trying to get in all afternoon, and your mother thinks they might find out this number. I've already had about fifty of them pretending to be you on the public hospital lines."

Despite everything, I gave a small smile. Trust my mother to come up with that. It was part of why she made a good queen. I would never have been able to keep my composure long enough to worry about secret questions.

"Go ahead."

He cleared his throat again. "What item of jewelry did your mother give to you last year?"

I looked down. It was still sitting around my neck. Now devoid of magic, it was nothing more than a beautiful pendant, but the Havfrue Ruby meant everything to me. I never took it off.

"It was a necklace with a ruby pendant."

"Yes, yes, well done." He answered me like I'd just won a competition rather than the ability to ask after my own father.

"So how is he?" I asked when it became apparent he'd completely forgotten why I'd called.

"Oh, yes. I'm afraid there is no change. I've got my best doctors with him, trying to diagnose the problem, and a team of the top specialists in every field are being called in from all over Trifork."

"Could it be a magical problem?"

"What?"

Magic was not common in Trifork. Unlike some of the other kingdoms, we had almost no magical people living here. Our only magic came from the depths of the ocean, and that strictly wasn't ours. It belonged to the merfolk of Havfrue.

"Magic. Could magic be causing his illness?"

"I'm afraid I can't possibly say. Do you think it might be a possibility?"

I thought back to the sea witch. Whatever Ari thought about it, I still wasn't sure she didn't have something to do with this. Ok, she'd been dead for months, but her magic lingered on, causing lasting damage to those affected. I knew she'd been planning to hurt my father before she died, so it wasn't beyond the realm of possibility that she'd managed to perform a spell on him before she became a shark's lunch.

"Yes, I do."

There was silence on the line, and for a second, I thought he might have been cut off, but then he answered me. "I'll have someone brought in from Thalia or one of the other magical kingdoms to check. They might be able to figure out the problem better than we seem to be doing."

I thanked him and hung up.

"How is he?" Ari asked his voice full of concern. He'd not touched his sandwich at all.

I picked mine up from the silver tray.

"He's the same," I replied. "They have people trying to figure it out. The head of medicine at the hospital is sending for some mages to help diagnose him."

"So I heard," Ari said, finally biting into his sandwich after seeing me take mine. "I think you are wrong, though. I'll be surprised if it turns out to be magic."

After we'd both eaten our sandwiches, I placed the tray back on my bedside cabinet and turned back to Ari. There was expectation in the air between us. I'd never slept with a boy in my room before. Not unless you counted Hayden who used to come to sleep-overs on my birthday with the rest of my classmates when we were little.

I leaned forward and kissed him. His lips were so warm and yet he still tasted of the ocean, even when he was away from it. It was a taste and a smell I associated with him without even thinking about it now. I could never go for a walk by the sea and smell the briny air without picturing Ari in my mind. He turned his body into me, and I heard him moan. At first, I thought it was a moan of pleasure. I'd certainly been enjoying myself, but when he pulled back quickly and gritted his teeth. I knew the pain was winning.

Grabbing the cream next to the silver tray, I squeezed the tube and applied liberal amounts of the stuff to his legs, hoping it would ease his pain. As I slathered it on, great globs of it fell onto the bed, messing my sheet up even further, not that I cared. A sheet could be washed.

He barely made a sound as I smoothed the cream on thickly, but he gripped the sheets beneath him and closed his eyes despite the deliberate lightness of my touch.

"Does it feel any better?" I asked. His legs were now wet and white, hiding the worst parts.

"A little..." he grimaced again as he tried to move on the bed to make space for me. "Ok, not much," he admitted.

I picked up the sleeping pills. They would knock him out almost instantly and keep him asleep for hours, but it was better than him lying next to me in agony. I couldn't bear it.

"No!" he growled when he saw what I'd picked up.

I sighed, knowing it was no use arguing with him. We were both going to have to sleep on wet sheets covered in skin cream and blood, with him not daring to move because of the pain moving would cause. I'd sleep so far on the edge of the bed for fear of hurting him in my sleep that it was more than a possibility I'd fall off.

As I replaced the bottle of pills, my eyes fell upon something else.

Picking up the salt shaker, I dashed into the bathroom and turned both taps on, emptying the whole shaker of salt into it.

"What are you doing?" I heard Ari call out.

"I'm making this night a whole lot easier for both of us," I grinned, poking my head back around the door.

It took a whole five minutes to get Ari from the bed to the bathtub, but the look of relief on his face as his legs turned back to a tail made it worth it.

"You can sleep in here." I pointed out.

"What about you?"

I thought about it. The bed would feel lonely, knowing Ari was in the next room. Besides, the sheets were totally ruined, and I didn't want to bother the staff any more than I had to. Instead, I brought a pillow from the bed and placed it beside the bathtub.

"I'm going to sleep right here next to you."

The way he looked at me then almost broke my heart. It was as if no one had ever done anything for him before. I could feel everything in that look, and I only wished that the bathtub was bigger so I could climb in with him.

It wasn't the way I'd expected to spend my first night sleeping with a man, but it was the only way that worked.

In the morning, I woke up to a neck so stiff that I could barely move it and the news that my father had died during the night. The new queen of Trifork had spent the night on the bathroom floor.

The New Queen

It was John that came to my room at five-thirty in the morning to inform me of the news. It was also John that held me as I cried. Ari, unable to move quickly thanks to having to wait for his tail to change into legs, only managed to get to me once my tears had subsided. John passed me over to him, and I clung to him, holding onto his naked body, covered only in a sheet as if he were the only thing that would stop me drowning in grief.

"I'll give you time to compose yourself, but I must inform Anthony of the news." John was ever the professional. I knew he was close to my father and would feel his passing almost as keenly as I had, and yet he stood at my door with the stoic composure I, as the new queen, should be showing.

"Would you like me to tell the staff or would you prefer to do that?"

I wiped a tear from my eye and looked up at him. I knew what he was really asking me. He was asking if I was strong enough to take on the duties I'd been training for my whole life. It was crunch time, and he was waiting to see if I'd sink or swim. I took a deep breath and pulled myself up to my full height.

"Please gather everyone into the great hall in thirty minutes. I'll tell everyone the news."

John nodded. He didn't smile. Of course, he didn't. There was nothing to smile about, but I saw the pride in his expression as he nodded his head and turned away.

"I need to get dressed," I said quickly, panic evident in my voice. "Something appropriate and formal...and black." I turned away from Ari to head to the closet, but he pulled me back toward him and held onto me, running his fingers through my hair with one hand and gripping me to him so tightly, my face was almost crushed to his chest.

I didn't want to break down. I'd already cried in front of John, but Ari was a cocoon wrapped around me. A safe harbor in the worst storm of my life and a haven of safety cushioning me from the reality I'd woken up to. I let the tears fall, creating streams down Ari's chest and over his stomach. I sobbed, letting all the pain out, and despite his own pain, Ari was a rock, holding me until I was completely out of tears. Letting go of him was hard. Like setting adrift, away from an anchored ship, but I had to go. I had a job to do, and people were counting on me.

"Stay here. There's no point you trying to walk. I'll come back for you."

Ari nodded, knowing that the best help he could be was to do as I asked. I pulled out a demure black dress from my closet and pinned my hair back from my face.

Ari gave me a quick kiss as I left the room. Downstairs, I found John in his office fielding calls from journalists and well-wishers. When he saw me walk in, he hung up midway through a conversation.

"Your Majesty." He bowed to me in a way he never had before. It was so poignant, and it didn't escape me that our relationship had changed overnight. I was no longer the princess. I was now the queen and, therefore, his boss.

As I had asked, the staff had congregated in the main hall. I think most of them had guessed the news I was about to tell them. I noticed a few had wet eyes as I made my way to the front. Anthony was already there, and as I took the stage, he took my hand. We were in this together, my brother and I.

"I'm afraid I have bad news," I said, keeping my voice even and trying to remember to breathe. "The king passed away overnight."

They knew the news was coming, and yet, they were as shocked as I had been. Many of them cried. Once I'd dismissed them, Anthony stepped up to speak to me.

"We need to make arrangements. The media will be out here in force, and we will need to tell them when and where the funeral will be. I'm sure John will help us with everything. The flag at the front of the palace needs to be lowered to half-mast, and the hospital needs a phone call to arrange for father's body to be picked up."

My mind was whirring with all the jobs I had to do. Each seemed more important than the last. When had Anthony grown up so much? He was more on top of everything than I was. I needed to pull myself together.

"Can you ask John to meet with us in his office in ten minutes to organize the funeral and press? I'll sort out everything else."

Anthony gave me a curt nod and left me alone in the great hall.

My first priority was to call the hospital. Not to make arrangements about my father's body, but to speak to my mother. She would be distraught and the thought of her there alone made me feel sick to my stomach.

On the way to the nearest phone, I spotted a maid.

"Please, can you arrange for the flag to be hung at half-mast and get someone from the kitchen to take some breakfast up to my room? Ari is there, and I'm sure he will be hungry."

"Yes, ma'am." The maid curtsied.

"And have some pastries and fruit brought to John's office too." I wasn't hungry, but Anthony and John might be.

The nearest phone was in a small office just off the main entrance hall. Thankfully, the office was empty. I picked up the phone and dialed carefully. When the head of staff answered, I asked to be put through to my mother, only to be informed that my mother had already left and was on her way home.

I'd hoped that would be all, but the head of staff wanted to know what to do with my father's body. I knew it was a job on my list, but I'd hoped John would deal with it. I had no idea what the protocol for the death of a sovereign was. My father's father died when I was just a baby.

"I'm not sure what the best course of action would be at the moment," I replied to him, but then he told me that the hospital was swarming with paparazzi and they needed it to be sorted out as quickly as possible.

The whole morning was a whirlwind of activity as John, Anthony, and I ran through everything that needed to be done. Thankfully, John did remember my grandfather's death and was able to get my father's body back here to the small chapel that sat in our grounds at the back of the palace without too much fuss.

Half an hour after I made the call to the hospital, my mother walked through the door surrounded by more guards than I'd ever seen before. Her face was blotchy from tears and for the first time ever, her hair was a mess. She was still wearing the same outfit she'd been wearing when she left in a rush the day before.

"Someone, get my mother a cup of tea," I shouted out, running over to her and enveloping her in a hug.

"No need. I'm tired. I'm going to retire to bed."

She did look tired. My mother, who always looked perfect, no matter the occasion, had big black circles under her eyes, eyes that were bloodshot and puffy.

I was about to argue that she shouldn't be on her own, but looking at the way she was, sleeping was probably the best thing she could do.

I walked with her up to her room and sat with her a while as she lay on the bed sobbing quietly. Eventually, the sobs subsided and were replaced with soft snoring. Wearily, I dragged myself from her room and headed back to John's office.

As I entered, Anthony and John were in deep conversation.

Pages and pages of paper covered the desk between them.

Anthony turned his head as I closed the door behind me. "We have made arrangements for father's funeral to be held in two weeks in the Trifork Minster."

"Two weeks? Isn't that a long time to wait?"

The thought of my father's body lying in the small chapel for so long made me feel numb.

"It's actually pretty quick for a head of state," John answered solemnly. "It's not like a normal funeral. There has to be a period of public mourning. The press in all the nine kingdoms need time to get their people here. We expect hundreds of thousands of mourners to show up and security needs to be put in place to keep everyone safe. We also have to send out the invites to the heads of state of other kingdoms. It is a massive undertaking. My office will be extremely busy, plus after that, there is the matter of your coronation. We can't leave too long a gap between both events."

Both events. It sounded like hc was talking about a couple of parties, not the burial of my father and the bonding of me to my kingdom.

The afternoon dragged on in a blur as I sifted my way through all the official paperwork that had to be taken care of, starting with developing the long list of names from which to choose whom to invite and organizing how we would handle the entire event in respect of the public and press.

Hours later, my stomach rumbled. I looked at the clock on the wall behind John. Due to my numb state and the fact that we'd been so busy, we'd managed to work straight through the whole day without pausing to eat. With a start, I realized I'd left Ari on his own in my room all day.

"You guys should eat," I said, jumping up out of my seat. I'll meet you back here in twenty minutes. There is something I have to do.

Without waiting for an answer, I dashed out the door and up the stairs.

"He's already left, ma'am." It was the same maid I'd spoken to earlier.

"When?" My heart sank. I couldn't believe I'd not thought to come visit him all day. I'd been so wrapped up in my own grief and duties that I'd not once thought to come and check on him.

"How did he leave? He can barely walk."

"He did walk, ma'am. I saw him go. He asked me to tell you that he'll see you later and he'll stay around the shoreline in case you need him."

I thanked her and hurried back down the stairs, feeling incredibly guilty.

Walking, even the short distance to the ocean without help would be agony for him. I wished he'd come to me and let me help him.

I saw my sheet caught on the rocks where he'd left it weighted down so it wouldn't fly away.

Picking it up, I called out to Ari.

Way behind me, on the public side of the promenade, I could hear the members of the press shouting my name. I turned to find literally hundreds of them, jostling for position to get the best photo of me.

I closed my eyes, feeling dizzy from lack of food and the weight of grief that pulled at my heart.

A splashing noise caused me to open my eyes. Ari appeared, his head and shoulders coming out of the water, his obsidian hair trailing behind him, and fanning out where it touched the sea.

"I'm so sorry," I began, kneeling and reaching out to him. "I didn't mean to leave you alone for so long. There was just so much to do, and everything is so overwhelming right now."

Ari held up his forefinger to my lips. I could taste the salty water that dribbled down over my chin.

He heaved himself up on the rock and kissed me. As he'd just come from the ocean, his face was wet, making me wet with it. Not that I cared. It was the first moment since I'd gotten out of bed that I'd didn't think of my father and of the million and one things I had to do. In that moment, there was just Ari and me.

Ari, me, and the thousand photographers taking our picture. A picture that would inevitably end up on the front page of the newspapers tomorrow.

"I understand," Ari said as he pulled back from me. I almost followed his lips which would have made me fall into the ocean with him. It was extremely tempting.

"You are going through a lot right now, and you have much to do. I'll always be here for you, and when you are able, we'll go back out to sea together."

I sighed. With the mountain of paperwork I had to wade through, going out to sea with Ari was a long way off.

"I don't think I'll be able to come out with you until all this dies down, but I promise to come visit you soon." I indicated the braying paparazzi mob behind me. Ari's eyes flicked to them for a moment then turned back to me.

"I don't care about them. I do, however, care about you. I will be waiting for you. I'm always here."

He kissed me again, this time quickly and disappeared under the water.

If my heart had felt empty before, it was even worse now. I was tired, right down to my bones. I couldn't exactly call my mother lucky, but at least she was allowed to sleep through everything. I'd give my right arm to be able to drift into sweet oblivion and wake up when this all didn't seem like such a nightmare.

Taking my sheet with me, I ambled back across the rocks, giving a small wave to the photographers. It didn't matter what I did. They already had the shot they wanted. However much I didn't like it, Ari and I were huge news. No doubt they'd make a big deal of me visiting him on the day my father died.

I was feeling very anti-media as I entered the house. John caught me as I'd just made it through the door. "I'm sorry Your Highness. I know you are tired, but the press is assembled in the grand hall. They want an official statement from the palace." He looked at me apologetically as I gawked back at him.

"Why? How?" I was so tired; I couldn't even articulate the words. I'd only been gone fifteen minutes, twenty at most. How had a press conference managed to be arranged and set up in such a short period of time?

"I'm most terribly sorry," John apologized again. "My staff set it up without my knowledge. We've been locked away all day, and they took it upon themselves to bring the press in. I shall turn them away immediately then reprimand my staff at once."

"No." I brought my hand up to my head where a headache was developing. My stomach also pained me because of not eating all day, but I couldn't just turn the media away. I needed to show the kingdom some leadership and sending the press away when the public needed me the most seemed the worst thing to do, "I'll speak to them. Please don't reprimand your staff. It was the right thing to do."

John gave me a small smile and nodded his head.

I turned to the double doors of the grand hall, and as I pushed them open, I realized I had not the first clue of what I was going to say.

Heartbreak

The month after my father's death passed incredibly slowly, and yet, every second of my day was accounted for. Every night, I flopped into bed and fell asleep almost before my head hit the pillow. Despite my promise to Ari, I'd not found time to visit him once. My heart burned with the pain of not seeing him, but there was always just one more speech to give, one more form to sign, one more person I had to deal with. The funeral had run as smoothly as could be expected, but my upcoming coronation was fraught with problems. Problems I didn't want to deal with. I didn't really want to deal with any of it. I needed to deal with my own grief, but like everything else, that was also something I didn't have time for. I'd known my father was a busy man, but it hadn't occurred to me just how busy he was.

As I had with Ari, I'd also had to push my other friendships to one side. Astrid and Hayden had postponed their wedding as they had said they would, and now the date was set at some vague point in the future. I think they were waiting until my coronation to set an actual date, but as I was putting it off as long as possible, their wedding was heading farther into the future. I felt so bad for them, but as I never could find the time to see them, I was unable to apologize in person.

"My whole life is wrapped up in queen stuff," I complained to my mother about six weeks after my father had died. She was brushing my hair at her large dressing table.

"It won't always be like this," my mother soothed. "When your father became king, I barely saw him for months, but then things settled down, and we were able to find some time together. The secret is delegating."

I looked at myself in the mirror. My mother had gone back to the well-dressed, perfect looking woman she had been before her husband died, but I looked like I hadn't slept in a month.

There were bags under my eyes, and my skin was almost gray in color. Even my hair that usually had a vibrant red hue was dull and lifeless.

It was easy for my mother to say I should delegate, but I already was delegating every task I could. John was doing twice the work he normally did, and his staff was coming in extra weekends to help prepare for the coronation. Anthony was going way above and beyond his duties by dealing with all the foreign issues—issues I should be dealing with myself but didn't really understand. I was left to deal with the media. A job which I hated above all other jobs. There were endless streams of interviews from every TV network and every newspaper in all the nine kingdoms. I couldn't back out of any of them because, according to public opinion, doing so would make me an uncaring leader.

"Apparently, if I don't give at least a billion interviews a day, the public will think I'm a bad queen."

"You don't want to pay too much attention to what the public thinks," my mother replied, yanking the brush through my knotty hair. "It will drive you insane. Your father didn't."

I sighed and rested my head in my arms, forcing my mother to stop doing what she was doing.

"You've not had a minute to yourself in weeks. You'll work yourself into the ground at this rate. How long has it been since you last saw Ari?"

She knew how long it had been. Over six weeks. I'd tried to get out of the palace on a number of occasions, but some emergency or other had always prevented me from leaving. When I closed my eyes at night, all I saw was him. I longed to be back out in the ocean, to be beside him once again.

"I thought so," my mother said, not waiting for a reply. "It's about time I gave an interview or two. I'll take over your duties today, and you can go for a swim."

I pulled my head up and looked at her reflection. She smiled at me with such warmth in her eyes.

"Thank you!" I jumped up, knocking the brush from her hand and turned to hug her. She was right. I did need a break.

"Go then, before I change my mind."

I kissed her cheek and ran from the room. As I passed John's office, I poked my head around the door and told him that my mother was taking all interviews this afternoon. He held two thumbs up and gave me a grin.

My heart already felt lighter as I dashed across the rocks. Not caring about the remaining paparazzi, I pulled my black dress over my head, and in only my underwear I dived right in.

I'd barely swum more than a couple of meters when I bumped right into my grandfather. As soon as he took my hand, I was able to breathe underwater like he did. If only I didn't have to hold onto a merperson to be underwater. It was so very inconvenient. He spoke to me through telepathy, the same way that Ari and I spoke when we were underwater. I could communicate this way with Ari because we had a special bond, but with my grandfather, it was all magic. Although he was nowhere near as powerful as the sea witch had been, magically speaking, he did have some powers. Being able to talk to me telepathically was one of them. The only problem was, beyond Ari and my grandfather, I wasn't able to talk to any of the other merfolk and the few times I'd been to Havfrue, I'd had to remain silent or try to communicate with a crude sign language.

Erica!" I've not seen you or your mother in weeks. I thought I'd come and pay a visit...What's the matter?

My tears were invisible under water. One lot of salty water pouring seamlessly into another, but I'm sure he picked up on the shock on my face. What with everything going on in the palace and in Trifork, I'd completely forgotten to tell my grandfather of my father's death. He wouldn't be upset, not in the traditional sense. My grandfather was my mother's father and had only met my father on a few occasions. He should have been told from a political perspective, though. *My father died.*

Now, it was my grandfather's turn to look shocked. Despite our rocky start, my grandfather had grown quite fond of me. He pulled me into his arms and almost engulfed me in a hug.

He was so young. How did it happen?

I shook my head, remembering back to when the doctors had told us the cause of death. It hadn't seemed real at the time. I wasn't sure I believed it now all these weeks later.

They said he had a viral infection that caused a heart attack, but I'm not so sure."

He narrowed his eyes. *What do you mean? You think there was more to it?*

I wasn't sure if I should tell him my suspicions. Everyone else I'd told thought I was crazy for even thinking it, but in my mind, it made total sense.

"I think the sea witch did it.

There, I'd said it. I waited for him to tell me I was stupid or wrong. Instead, he looked at me closely.

She's dead. Make no mistake, my pet finished her off.

The pet he talked about was a huge shark he kept in his underwater palace.

I know that, but isn't it possible that she cast some sort of spell before she was killed? She was certainly planning to kill my father, she told me.

She told you right before being eaten by a shark. I doubt she'd have time to finish any spells. I think that sometimes things are just as they seem. If your medics think your father died of natural causes, then maybe you should believe them.

Easy to say, but the problem was, I didn't believe it. The spell on Ari had not been broken, and I'd heard that the same could be said for others in Havfrue. My father was so young and vibrant. Was it really possible that a viral infection had killed him?

How is your mother holding up? I must go and see her.

She's doing as well as can be expected. Today she's speaking to the media for the first time since he died.

My grandfather nodded his head thoughtfully. *And how are you doing? This must have come as a huge shock to you. You'll be queen now, right? That's a big responsibility for someone as young as you. Do you need me to come up to the palace and help in any way?*

My heart lifted as I mulled over his offer. He'd become quite a celebrity in Trifork when the media first found out about him, and being a private man, he didn't like the intrusion. That's why he only visited once in a while. Coming up to the palace to help was a generous offer and who better to help me be a queen than a man who was a king?

I kissed his cheek and smiled. My first smile in weeks. *Thank you, I'd love that. Before we go home, I was wondering if you'd help me with one thing first.*

Anything.

I looked out into the vast ocean. I knew Havfrue was there, but it was a long way for anyone to swim without a tail.

Would you take me to Havfrue? It will be so much quicker with your help.

My grandfather's lips curled up at the edges. *Would this be anything to do with that young man of yours by any chance?*

Even in the cool water, I could feel the blush rise to my cheeks.

I' haven't seen him in six weeks. The pressures of becoming queen have taken all of my time.

I felt a jerk as my grandfather set off, pulling me at high speed behind him. Without him, the journey would take me, at least, half an hour, and I'd have to battle the waves. With him pulling me underwater, we made the journey in less than ten minutes. Of course, I could have called out for Ari to come to me, but this way I'd be able to surprise him. I pointed out the avenue that Ari lived on and let my grandfather swim me along it. Every merperson we met bowed as we passed.

Anticipation of finally seeing him again made me both nervous and excited. I could feel my heart lifting just by the fact I was closer to him. Being bonded to him and living so far apart was difficult and it was only now as we got close to his house that I realized just how heavy my heart had become. I'd thought it was grief and stress, and probably a lot of it was, but being away from Ari only compounded it all, making me feel I was walking around with weights on my shoulders.

Havfrue houses do not have windows and doors in the same way we do on land. They had the openings, but no glass and no doors. Water flowed freely through all the openings. It meant there was very little privacy, but at least, you got to see the brightly colored fish without having to leave your home.

My heart was positively bursting with joy as we came up to his house. The downside of being apart from Ari was the pain and heaviness of my heart but on the flipside, being so close to him was like I was walking on air. I didn't even need to see him to feel it. The joy was already coursing through my veins as we stopped at his house.

A small creature swam through his window and wrapped itself around my arm.

"Ollie!" I cried out, using my mouth and sending bubbles of air up to the surface. Ollie was Ari's pet octopus. I stroked his head and then peeked in the window opening. All at once, the happy feelings I'd been experiencing fell like a ton of bricks. I pulled my grandfather away from the window. I didn't want him to see what I'd just seen.

Isn't he home? asked my grandfather in confusion.

He's home alright. Home with another girl!

A Hurried Wedding

I don't know how I managed to get home. My entire world had come crashing down around me. If it wasn't bad enough that I'd just lost my father, it seemed that I'd lost Ari too. I knew heartbreak was never easy, but the fact we were bonded made it a bitter pill to swallow.

"She might have just been a friend," My grandfather offered as he pulled us both out of the water by the rocks. The photographers were still out in force, managing to get a photo of me looking absolutely dreadful in my underwear and tears streaking down my face.

I ignored everyone and headed straight to bed, hiding myself under my duvet and getting my pillow wet as I'd not bothered to dry my hair. Someone knocked on my door, but I was in no mood to speak to anyone. I felt numb and empty, and I was going to be no use to John or anyone else in the state I was in.

Every time I closed my eyes, I could see him with her. She had long flowing yellow hair. Not blond but an acidic looking bright yellow. My grandfather had asked if I'd got the wrong idea, and they were just friends, but I'd seen him lean forward and kiss her. Friends didn't kiss each other in their own homes when they thought no one was watching.

I spent the night revolving between blaming myself for not finding time to go see him and wanting to rip his head off for cheating on me.

Ok, it could be argued that we were not officially a couple. We'd both known that it couldn't last forever, but I'd not thought it would end so soon, and with betrayal. In my heart, I'd hoped there would be a happy ending for us, a way to get past the problems we faced, but in my head, I knew our relationship had to come to an end at some point.

In the morning, I was a complete wreck. I'd barely slept at all, and the bags under my eyes had taken on such epic proportions, that I was sure they were going to overbalance me. There was another knock on the door, and this time, I answered it. I opened the door to my mother staring at me, her mouth hanging open in shock.

"Erica! You look dreadful! What's this in your hair?" She pulled something green and stringy from my hair that turned out to be seaweed.

"Go in the shower and get yourself dressed," she demanded. She didn't like me to look anything other than the princess I was...correction, the queen I was.

I looked down at my underwear. It had dried overnight but had salt stains all over it from the sea water. I turned and padded into my bathroom, turning the bath on instead of the shower. If I had a shower, she'd expect me out in minutes. This way I'd at least get half an hour or so to myself. At least, I thought I would. I wasn't prepared for her following me in and sitting by the side of the bath.

"Can't a girl get some privacy around here?" I muttered. I wanted to wallow in my own despair, and I could hardly do that with my mother watching. She passed me a shampoo bottle.

"Father told me what happened," she began, pouring shampoo liberally over my head when I didn't take the bottle from her. "I'm so sorry Erica. I thought he was such a nice boy once I got to know him."

I didn't answer. What was there to say? Instead, I elected to lose myself in the feeling of her massaging the shampoo into my scalp the way she did when I was a little girl. I could hear her talking, but the scalp massage was making me sleepy.

"Erica!"

I nodded awake abruptly. I'd completely fallen asleep in the tub. Water cascaded down over my ears as my mother rinsed out the shampoo.

"I'm sorry, I didn't sleep very well."

She sighed loudly behind me. "My father is here. He says he'll stay for a few days to help. Why don't you take a few days off work?"

I shook my head. "I can't. I'm the queen. I'm not allowed to be tired or sad or overwhelmed. I have to be regal and pretty and commanding and a million other things I fear I'll never be."

"You are so much more than you think you are. Take a week off. There will be plenty of time for you to be regal and commanding."

The thought of slouching around in my bed, not having to talk to anyone was appealing. In the end, I let my mother have her way. She got a maid to change the sheets on my bed, and I went into hibernation, not leaving my room until I could hide no more.

On the fifth day, when I'd cried more tears than I thought it possible, I got up, put on a dress and makeup and stepped out of my room. When I'd been with Ari, I was a princess, a girl. Now I was the queen, and I had a kingdom to run. Heartbreak didn't fit into it at all. With purposeful strides, I marched to John's office. Anthony and my grandfather were there, deep in conversation. They all paused as I walked through the door.

"John, how are my coronation plans coming? I want to become the queen officially as soon as possible."

John gave a cough to clear his throat. "I'm sorry Your Highness, but after your father's funeral, the road outside the Minster began to crumble from the sheer number of people turning out to give their condolences. There is a team working on it right now, but it seems that the minster also needs some restorative work and they are doing it all at the same time to minimize the impact on people."

I sighed in frustration. I needed something to take my mind away from everything that had happened in the last few weeks, and I figured a coronation would do that, not to mention ruling a kingdom.

"How long until we can get in?" I sensed by the look on his face that I was not going to like his answer.

"We are going to have to put it back at least a couple of months, Your Highness."

A couple of months! That felt like an eternity away. "It will be getting cold by then. Winter will be creeping in."

"That's true, but a little snow won't stop us."

No, just a construction crew it seemed.

The weeks following were a mess of me trying to keep everything together on the outside while I was falling apart on the inside. I was lucky to have such a great support system behind me. John and Anthony helped with running the kingdom the best they could. My mother took over the planning of the coronation, and I spent umpteen hours giving interviews for the media, trying not to look like I had a stone in my chest where my heart once was.

A month after I'd seen Ari with the other girl, I finally canceled any more interviews. The reporters had gone from wanting to know about the kingdom and my place in it as queen to throwing in question after question about Ari's and my relationship.

After the last one where the reporter had refused point blank to leave until I answered his question about where Ari was, I'd had him thrown out and canceled everything else. It was ridiculous that everyone but me was actually doing the running of the kingdom and I spent my days fending off questions about my love life.

I made up my mind to spend more time with John and Anthony and actually make plans for the future of Trifork. I'd set off towards John's office when Astrid and Hayden collared me. Like everyone else that wasn't essential to running a kingdom, I'd barely seen them in months.

I took them into the small dining room where I instructed a maid to bring us some tea. Just being around them again brought some sense into my cluttered mind. I'd forgotten what it was like to just hang with my best friends and how easy it was to talk about things other than Trifork.

"How have you both been?" I asked uncertainly. I felt that I'd missed out on so much and, once again, had guilt that I'd pushed them to one side to figure out how to run the kingdom.

I saw a look pass between them, and for the first time since they'd got together, I felt like an outsider. Of course, I was always the third wheel in the relationship, but I'd never really felt that way...not until now.

"What is it?"

"It's the wedding," Astrid blurted out. "We want to ask your permission for it to go ahead."

She looked at me so expectantly that I almost cried. It broke my heart that they felt the need to ask my permission. I might be the queen, but I wasn't in charge of their lives any more than I was in charge of any of my other subjects' lives.

I took her hands in mine, then let one drop so I could reach out for Hayden's hand too.

"I'm so sorry. I haven't been a good friend to either of you recently."

"It's alright," Astrid replied earnestly. "We know you've been through a lot. We didn't want to ask you, but you are still chief bridesmaid, and we know the coronation is coming up."

I sighed. I'd never be coronated the way things were going. I was the queen, but I felt like I was still in limbo until it was made official.

"As long as you don't plan to marry at the Trifork Minster, you certainly can get married."

Astrid tightened the grip on my hand and grinned, and beside her, Hayden let out a sigh of relief.

"We don't actually have a venue planned yet. It wouldn't have been the Minster though. It's reserved for royalty, remember?"

Of course, it was. "I was joking. Of course, you guys should marry." I looked around the dining room. It was the smaller of the two the palace had, this one being reserved for family meals, but it was beautiful as was the rest of the palace.

"Why don't you get married here in the palace? You kinda almost did once already, and we have the space for as many guests as you like."

Astrid gazed around the room. I could see that she was weighing the possibility.

Hayden didn't need to look around.

He'd spent much of his childhood in this palace playing silly games like hide and seek with me. He knew what the place looked like already. "Actually I had an idea I'd like to run past you."

"Shoot."

"I was thinking we could borrow one of your da...your ships. I want to marry at sea."

This was obviously news to Astrid as much as it was to me. Her eyes widened, and she let out a squeal. I felt the corners of my mouth lift at her obvious excitement. It was the first time I'd smiled in so long, I was sure I'd forgotten how to do it.

"Of course. I'll secure one of the nicer ships for you. I'll need to know how many guests you want."

Hayden smiled as Astrid jumped up out of her seat and hugged me.

"Thank you. Thank you so much!" She turned to Hayden. "We can get married whenever we like. Let's do it next week. We already have the dresses."

Hayden shook his head. "What about the catering and the cake? It could take weeks to organize everything."

I began to panic. If they accidentally set their wedding on the same day, or even the same week as the coronation, I wouldn't be able to attend, and if I was going to be very honest with myself, I knew which I'd prefer to go to. Suddenly, a thought occurred to me. I could manage to sort out their wedding within a week, which would still give me at least three weeks to go before the coronation.

"My kitchen staff can cater your wedding. I have the finest chefs in the whole of Trifork working down there. I think they'll enjoy doing something more interesting than bringing me the occasional sandwich."

Hayden squeezed my hand and thanked me as Astrid stood up quickly.

"If the wedding is next week, I need to plan everything. Thank you, Erica." She kissed me on the cheek, and after another brief kiss, this time directed at Hayden, she dashed out the door.

I grinned at Hayden. Astrid's excitement was catching, pulling a load from my aching heart. "You might want to tell her she can also use the beauticians and hairdressers my mother hires. She'll never find anyone else at this late notice."

"Thank you, I will." Hayden moved forward and took both my hands in his. "How are you doing, Erica?"

"I'm fine," I lied.

As usual, Hayden saw right through it.

"No you aren't, and I don't expect you to be. I'm sorry about this whole wedding thing. It's just that with everything going on, it felt as though it might never happen at all."

"Don't be sorry. I'm excited for you both." I looked right at him. I could see right into his very soul and knew exactly what he was thinking. He felt sorry for me. He knew I'd turn up without a plus one, and he knew that all eyes would be on me rather than Astrid. Perhaps that's why he chose to have the ceremony so far away from prying eyes. If we were on a boat so far out to sea, the media would find it hard to follow us. I guess they could hire boats themselves, but we'd be inside, not on deck and therefore any photos they took would be pointless.

"Ari is an idiot. A total, complete, and utter ass to let you go."

I smiled again, but this time it was full of sadness. Hayden's words were all well and good, but the truth was that Ari had let me go. He'd discarded me for someone better, someone easier...someone with a tail and he'd not even had the balls to come tell me face to face.

"It doesn't matter. I'm over it. How many people are you expecting to come to the wedding?" I changed the subject quickly, hoping that he wouldn't bring up Ari again. I didn't want to talk about him, at least, not with Hayden.

Hayden stared back at me, his eyes unblinking. "It does matter Erica. Of course, it matters. You've been through so much in such a short time, and then that unfeeling cad goes and does that to you? If I could swim underwater, I'd go down there and..."

I gave a small laugh. The whole thing was moot. Hayden couldn't swim underwater, so there was no point talking about it.

"There's nothing you can do, and I don't need you to fight my battles for me. The past is the past, and it's the future of Trifork I have to look out for now."

Hayden brought himself closer to me and wrapped his arms around me tightly. I held myself together. I'd shed enough tears, and it was about time I grew up.

Two Jobs and a Blind Date

The very next morning, the opportunity for me to do just that arose in a most unexpected way. I was having breakfast alone in the small dining room when my mother joined me.

"Can I have some more food, please?" I asked the maid as my mother took a seat beside me.

"Just coffee will be good, thanks," my mother said to the maid's back as she retreated. After turning to me, she added, "I'm not feeling too hungry. I've been thinking about your coronation."

"Hmmm," I answered, taking a bite out of a croissant smothered in jam.

"There is still time to find someone. John tells me that it has been put back again which makes me think that fate is working in your favor."

I knit my brows together, not comprehending at all what she meant.

"Find someone for what?" I asked flakes of pastry dropping from my mouth. I picked up my napkin and dabbed my mouth waiting for an inevitable reprimand for not eating in a ladylike manner.

When she answered, it was much worse than a telling off.

"A partner... a man to stand by your side as you walk up the aisle."

"You want me to find a man and marry him before my coronation? It hasn't been put off that long."

She gave me one of her stern looks. "Don't be silly, dear. I'm not suggesting you marry someone...not right away, anyway, but it's a difficult job, ruling a kingdom, and I'd like to think you'll have some help."

"I have help," I argued back. "I have John and Anthony and you."

"Yes, and I'm sure we'll help in whatever way we can, but you'll need the emotional support only a partner can give. It's a lonely life being queen and once you officially take that title, finding a man will drop to a very low priority.

Why not do it now and get it over and done with?"

Get it over and done with? She made it sound like a trip to the dentist but a whole lot less appealing.

She took my silence as me thinking about it and continued. "I know you had a thing for Ari. He was a nice boy, well, until...you know. It's Hayden and Astrid's wedding next week. Will you think about taking someone as a date?"

I raised a brow and tried to keep a lump in my throat from cutting off my airway at the mention of Ari. "You just said it yourself. It's next week. Seven days away. The only guys I've ever known are Ari and Hayden, and I'm pretty sure Astrid wouldn't take kindly to me asking Hayden as my date to his own wedding."

She waved her hand in my direction. "Stop it. I have someone for you to take. He's a nice young man from a good family."

"Fine!" I replied, standing up from the table. I hated the fact that the mere mention of Ari had my heart feeling like a stone was squeezing my chest. I needed to think about something...or someone else. Besides, I didn't have the energy to argue with her about it.

"Don't you want to know about him?" she asked as I headed for the door.

"Not especially." I figured I'd find out when I met the guy, and I couldn't for the life of me think that I'd be interested in him at all. It was easy for my mother to throw men my way, just as it was easy for me to say that I was over Ari, but the truth was that I wasn't over Ari. Nowhere near it.

"His name is Josh!" she called out as I left the room.

She spent the rest of the week in a complete panic, having taken it upon herself to organize the wedding as well as my coronation. She complained at every given opportunity about the shortness of time she had to prepare everything, although everyone knew she relished the responsibility. She knew how to throw a great party which was just as well, really, as my only contribution to the big day was to make sure one of my ships was in dock at the right time.

I spent the week trying not to think about either Ari or this Josh person

On the day itself, I left Anthony and John in charge and headed down to the main hall where my mother had told me to go.

The entire place was a hive of activity, with all the food from the kitchens being brought up on trays covered in film to keep the air getting to them. Various staff members bustled about picking them up one by one and taking them someplace through one of the doors.

"Where are they going?" I wondered aloud.

"Ah there, you are. Come over here." My mother appeared at my side and took my hand, leading me to the last seat in a row. She looked a little peaky which was hardly a surprise. She'd barely stopped since the wedding was announced. If I'd put in the amount of effort she'd done to make this wedding a huge event, I'd probably have died of exhaustion. I was tired just thinking about it.

The bridesmaids each had a seat, and both Astrid's and Hayden's mothers were seated on the other end, gossiping while a team of hairdressers and beauticians worked on them. My mother pushed me into the chair beside the one occupied by Astrid and beckoned one of the beauticians over.

Astrid already had her hair done. The blue-green waves she usually wore had been pinned back in a half updo. Her hair still cascaded down her back, but it was pulled back out of her face with a diamond hair clip.

They'd just started working on her face, but she didn't need makeup, she was naturally beautiful.

"You could go as you are and still be the most beautiful woman in the place," I commented as a woman with a comb and pair of scissors attacked my unruly hair.

Astrid glanced my way and grinned. "Don't be trying to upstage me, Erica."

"You need some color to balance the green hair," added the makeup artist who was in the process of painting her lips. "Otherwise you'll look washed out."

I wanted to point out that I was only joking, but I had a feeling that the woman wouldn't care.

When we were all finished, a large mirror was brought out to us so we could see ourselves. The food had already been delivered to the ship as had a huge sailor-themed cake I'd seen the servants walk past us with, so we were left alone to dress.

Astrid looked simply stunning in her nautical-themed dress paired with a veil made of netting. On anyone else, her outfit would have looked weird, but on her it was perfect. It suited her personality to a tee. Beside her, I scrubbed up pretty well myself.

Astrid draped her hand across my shoulder. "I can't believe I'm getting married today. I'm so glad I could share this day with you. I only wish..."

She didn't have to finish the sentence for me to know what it was she wanted to say. She wished I had someone, Ari perhaps. I hadn't told her about Josh. I'd spent the week trying not to feel dread about my upcoming blind date. It was something I'd regretted saying yes to ever since I had done it.

"I'm just amazed Hayden could find someone who'd stay with him," I teased. She gave me a playful pat on the arm.

As I gazed at the pair of us in the mirror, I had a flash of myself in a wedding dress standing next to Ari. If I could have moved my legs more than a couple of inches in the mermaid dress Astrid had put me in, I would have tried to kick myself.

"No more dilly-dallying, you two. It's time to go." My mother herded us all out of the grand hall to a waiting bus. It was painted white, and the windows were covered so no one could take a sneaky photo of us.

"We are going on a bus?" I arched an eyebrow at my mother who was busy ushering the younger bridesmaids onboard.

"What else would have gotten us of all to the dock? I've arranged a tent for us to drive into to walk through to get onto the ship so the media doesn't catch sight of the bride."

As usual, she'd thought of everything. I held Astrid's hand as we completed the small journey, each of us lost in our own thoughts. The tent my mother had mentioned was more of a fabric walkway from one end of the dock where we parked the bus, to the ship itself.

Once inside the ship, we were shown to the captain's quarters, while the guests and Hayden were in the main hall of the ship waiting for us, presumably along with the mysterious Josh. We had no fixed destination, but the plan was to sail for an hour until the shore was barely visible and perform the ceremony there. It was so romantic. The windows onboard were also covered to stop the media from getting any photos just as they had been on the bus. It made sense, but it also meant I couldn't see where we were going. I was going to miss out on watching the sea below us.

As the ship began to move, I felt a small thrill of panic. The last time I'd been on a ship as big as this, it had gone down in a storm created by the sea witch. I told myself that the witch was dead, and no storms had been forecast, but I couldn't help feeling that I was putting myself in danger. I looked across to my mother. She obviously felt the same way. Having not been out to sea in eighteen years due to her fear of water, this was a momentous occasion for her. Not even since she found out about the sea witch's demise had she ventured out into the water. I felt such pride watching how well she was handling it even though she looked a little green around the gills so to speak.

"I have a gift for you," Astrid said excitedly pushing a gift-wrapped circular box into my hands and taking my attention away from my mother.

"I wasn't expecting a gift," I replied, looking down at the exquisitely wrapped box with a blue ribbon around it. "Aren't I supposed to be the one giving you a gift?"

"There's been a slight change of plans."

I gave her a quizzical look. Change of plans? "What do you mean?"

"Just open it!" She was practically jumping up and down with excitement. Whatever was in the box must be good.

I opened it quickly, throwing the wrapping on the floor and eliciting a stern look from my mother in the process. Inside the box was a top hat. I pulled it out, wondering if there was anything else, but beneath the hat, the box was empty.

"I don't get it!"

"You are my chief bridesmaid." She rocked forward and backward on her heels, barely containing her excitement.

"I know," I answered slowly, wondering where this was leading and what possible use I could have for a top hat.

"But you are also Hayden's best man."

I looked at her quizzically.

"Think about it," she continued, taking the hat from my hands and placing it lightly atop my head so as not to mess up my hairdo. "He's your best friend. Who else would he choose? We both wanted you, but instead of arguing who should get you, we decided to share."

I laughed at her. This was the most untraditional wedding I'd ever been to. I loved it! If it wasn't for everything else going on in my life and the fact I had a blind date coming up, I'd have almost felt happy. The weight on my chest lifted as I took in her expression.

"Ok, I'm up for it. Does this mean I should go down to the hall?" I asked, unsure of what exactly my duties were now.

"Go!" she grinned at me, shooing her hands in my general direction.

As I headed for the door, I caught a glimpse of my mother. She looked even worse than she had before, and I wondered if it was possible for mermaids to get seasick. As I headed down the stairs to join Hayden, my heart inexplicably soared. The weight on my chest, which had lifted slightly whcn Astrid passed me my top hat, was now gone completely leaving me feeling as light as a feather. It was a curious feeling to have, seeing as only moments before sadness had been fighting for dominance over the fear of having to come up with small talk for my blind date.

It was then that I realized we'd be passing over Havfrue about now. The happiness I was feeling was only partly to do with Astrid and Hayden. No. The sudden lurch of my heart was because I was the closest I'd been in weeks to the man I was bonded to. However the magic worked, it was doing its job now, making me feel giddy and slightly sick. Directly below me, he would be there with his new girlfriend. Just like that, my heart changed direction and plummeted downward.

I sucked in a deep breath to center myself and opened the doors to the main hall. All at once, a hundred heads turned to look my way. As they began to stand, I realized that they thought Astrid was on her way.

"No! Sit down. I'm not a bridesmaid!" I hurried up the aisle, flapping my arms in a downward motion to get them all to sit. "I'm the best man!" I added, feeling somewhat foolish.

"Nice entrance, Erica. Subtle!" Hayden grinned as I took a spot by his side.

I threw him a dirty look and smoothed down my dress. "Have you got the rings? Because up until two minutes ago, I didn't even know I was doing this job." I hissed in his ear.

I kept my voice low, aware that there were rows and rows of people eagerly awaiting the bride within earshot. I glanced up at them, seeing a general state of confusion with some people sitting back down, and some still standing, unsure of what they were supposed to do.

"She'll be coming when the music starts," I pointed out. About halfway back next to the aisle, a young man with dirty-blond hair and steel gray eyes winked at me. I opened my mouth in shock at his rudeness but was then elbowed by Hayden, trying to get my attention.

As I looked over at him, he tapped his top pocket where there was a square bulge. He pulled out the ring box and handed it to me. As I had no pockets on the dress, I had to hold onto it.

"Thank you," Hayden whispered as the wedding march began to play. Astrid glided up the aisle like the crazy green-haired angel she was, followed by the rest of the bridesmaids. As she got to the front, she passed me my lilies and pulled my hat from my head. I guess I was back to being chief bridesmaid again.

The ceremony went beautifully, and once it was over, the food was brought out. My heart jumped all over the place, vacillating between extreme joy and sadness. I couldn't keep myself together, my brain in one place. Even throughout the speeches of which I now had two to give, my mind kept flowing back to Ari no matter how hard I tried to keep him out of it.

"You should start dating again," my mother commented once I'd sat back down.

Oh crap. I'd completely forgotten about my blind date. So it seemed had my mother even though she was the one who'd set the whole thing up. With any luck, she'd forgotten. She had a glass of champagne next to her that hadn't been touched, but the way she sounded when she spoke made me think that the glass was not her first. Her words were slurred. Only slightly, but I picked up on it. She had gone from green to gray in color and didn't look too well.

"Are you feeling alright?" I asked her, wondering if it was the fear of the ocean or the alcohol that was making her appear the way she did.

"I'm fine, just a bit overwhelmed. I have a bit of a headache," she replied, the slur much more prominent this time. I pulled the champagne away from her.

"I saw a bed in the captain's quarters. Maybe you should lie down for a while."

She looked like she was about to argue but then nodded. "Maybe you are right. I've felt better."

As I helped her back up the stairs to the captain's quarters, she mentioned me dating again.

"So Hayden is married...and not to you."

"Please don't start. You know that Hayden and Astrid are perfect for each other. Not that I was ever interested in the first place."

"I'm not starting anything," she argued. I noticed that she was leaning on me more and more heavily with each step. Just how much had she had to drink?

"But you will be the official ruler of Trifork soon, and you'll find it much easier with a man by your side. Your father always told me that he wouldn't be able to do it without me."

I didn't doubt her. They made a wonderful team. I thought back to John and Anthony back at the palace, taking over my role while I was here partying on a boat. At the moment, they were my team.

"What do you say?" she added as I opened the door to the captain's room.

"I'll think about it," I answered. She already knew this. Something was making her forgetful.

I left her there and headed up to the deck. Before the wedding, we'd all had to stay inside, but now that it was over, I was perfectly free to watch the water outside. I took a deep breath, filling my senses with the briny smell of the ocean I loved so much and pulled my tight dress up to the knee and stepped up onto the bottom railing to really feel the breeze on my face. Even without Ari, I would still have wanted to jump overboard, to feel the freedom of the vast ocean. Of course, I didn't. It would only mean disrupting the wedding not to mention ruining the dress I was wearing.

"Don't jump!"

Before I'd even had a chance to look behind me, I felt two arms circling my waist, tugging me from the railing. I let go, and the pair of us fell backward onto the deck, with me landing on top of whoever it was.

"You idiot!" I turned my head to find the man with the gray eyes who had winked at me earlier. So now he was not only rude, he was stupid too. I peeled myself off him and righted myself on the deck.

"I wasn't suicidal! I was enjoying the sea air!"

He sat up straight, putting his hands behind him. "Oh, I knew that, but I couldn't miss an opportunity to grab hold of our new queen. It's not often opportunities like that present themselves."

I opened my mouth, unable to formulate the words I needed to tell him what an odious ass he was. He'd gone beyond rude and straight into creepsville. I was about to blast him with some choice words when he held both hands up.

"I'm kidding. I'm sorry. Of course, I thought you were going to commit suicide. You were standing on the railing looking like you were about to leap over. My reaction was just instinct. I could hardly let the new queen kill herself, could I? I'd rather have made a mistake, which it seems in this case, I did, than not do anything and watch the future of Trifork's monarchy off herself and not do anything about it."

My hands went to my hips. I guess he had a point. I was leaning right over the railings, and to a passerby, it might have looked more sinister than it actually was.

He stood up and held his hand out. I deliberated on ignoring him but decided to give him the benefit of the doubt and shook his hand.

"I'm Josh by the way. I believe this is our hook-up."

I cringed at his choice of words.

"Do you not know who you are talking to?"

He ran his hands through his hair, letting it flop back to where it was before and gave me another wink. "Of course, I do. Sorry, am I supposed to bow?"

I could see he was challenging me. In all my television interviews in the past few weeks, I'd made it quite clear that I wasn't a fan of being bowed or curtseyed to and as queen I was going to phase the practice out except on special occasions. There was no doubt in my mind he'd seen them.

"It is customary," I replied, not looking him in the eye. He was far too good-looking for his own good, and those pale of eyes of his unnerved me a little. It was like he could look right through me.

He nodded his head slightly, and then with as much flourish as he could get away with, he gave me a very deep bow, his right arm around his middle and his left extended behind him. I felt my cheeks go red as a couple of wedding guests came through the door. They took one look at Josh and me and headed straight back inside.

"Get up, you oaf." I grabbed his hand and pulled him into an upright position. "I don't want to sound like a bore, but winking at me is not acceptable. You should also refer to me as Your Highness until my coronation, and then, I should be addressed as Your Majesty."

I could hear the words coming from my mouth and hated myself for saying them. If Hayden could hear me now, he'd think I was being a pompous idiot. No doubt, he'd find this whole situation funny.

"Ok, Your Highness, would you like to accompany me inside for a dance? That is, if that's acceptable behavior?"

I was just about to tell him where he could shove his dance when a familiar feeling came over me. My heart swelled making me feel almost giddy. I only ever felt this way when Ari was near. It was part of the bonding. I didn't even need to see him in order for him to have an effect on me.

I held onto the rail and looked over the side, to where the boat met the water causing foamy waves and sea spray. To my utter shock, I saw a merperson keeping up with the boat. Long black hair fanned out in the water behind him. I didn't need him to look up to know it was Ari.

The Adventurer

My heart racing was a direct result of Ari being there, but seeing him had only made it worse. I had no idea how he knew where I was, but it was no coincidence he'd chosen this ship to swim next to. As far as I was aware, he wasn't in the habit of following ships for no reason.

I opened my mouth to shout down to him, but then closed it as I found that I didn't know what to say to him. What was there to say to the person you thought was your soul mate, the man you were magically bonded to for life and yet had chosen another woman...correction... a mermaid over you?

He looked up causing me to step back. I didn't want him to see me. I didn't want to see his face. I couldn't bear it. My heart was happy he was nearby thanks to our bonding, but my soul was tired. Tired and scared. I don't even know what it was I was scared of, but it was definitely fear coursing through my veins, making my breaths come heavily as I backed towards the door of the ship.

"I'd love to dance," I said, turning to Josh. He appeared taken aback by words which was hardly a surprise given our inauspicious start. I held my hand out to him, trying not to think of Ari, and we both headed back indoors to the wedding party. I felt upset and angry with myself for my sharp reaction to seeing Ari. I was dripping with sweat, and my hand trembled in Josh's. He was so arrogant that he probably thought this reaction was all about him.

People had already begun dancing. Astrid and Hayden were in the center having a whale of a time if the looks of pure joy on their faces were anything to go by.

My plan had been to quietly slip away from Josh and head back to my seat, probably drinking all the champagne I could get my hands on, but Josh had other ideas. He spun me around, right onto the dance floor and held me tight so I couldn't escape.

I closed my eyes and gave in to it. Josh was a very skilled dancer, and it was obvious he'd taken years of dance lessons. It made me wonder what it was that he did. My mother had only told me that he came from a good family, and I'd elected not to listen to anything else. As we twirled around the dance floor, images of Ari crept into my mind. He'd been a great dancer too. That one time we'd danced together outside my palace had been amazing, but unlike Josh, his skill had come straight from the spell of the sea witch.

I couldn't bear it anymore. I could still feel him swimming close by. I opened my eyes to banish thoughts of him from my brain and gazed at Josh instead. I didn't like the man, but I couldn't deny how cute he was. In another life, I might have fallen for him.

"What is it you do?" I asked him, genuinely intrigued.

"You wouldn't believe me if I told you," he replied, annoying me further.

"Just tell me," I insisted, waiting for the lie to spill from his lips. I hadn't met many men in my time, but I already knew enough to know that Josh was a cad. Unless he told me he did nothing but live off his parent's money, I wasn't going to believe anything he said.

"I'm a treasure hunter."

And there it was. I wasn't surprised by the lie, just the magnitude of it. What a whopper.

"Actually, I'm a magical treasure hunter."

"Of course, you are," I replied, playing along. "I bet you rescue maidens from towers and fight dragons too."

"Sometimes. Mostly it's not as exciting as you'd imagine, but yeah, I've fought a few dragons in my time. I've befriended a few too. They aren't all bad."

I nodded, a fake smile plastered to my lips. The audacity of this guy was shocking. My heart was beating so hard thanks to Ari being in the vicinity, that I was beginning to feel a little overwhelmed.

Thankfully, the song that was playing came to a close allowing me the excuse to finish the dance.

"Thank you so much for the dance Josh, but if you'll excuse me, I really should mingle with the other guests."

He gave me a small smile and bowed his head, thankfully, not in the same way he had outside. I left his side and headed to a group of people who included Hayden's father and some of his navy buddies. When I was sure that Josh wasn't watching me anymore, I retreated back to my seat at the head table. My mother's glass of champagne still sat there, so I picked it up and drank it down quickly, following it up with my own. I wasn't strictly supposed to get drunk, but I needed something to calm my heart rate down, and a buttload of alcohol seemed the best way to go about it.

The rest of the party sped by in a whirl as my brain refused to let go of the image of Ari swimming beside us. So many questions were running through my mind. Why was he here? What did he want? Did he want to get back with me? Was he going to lie to me about the girl? All these thoughts rolled around in my head as the people around me danced and drank champagne and had a wonderful time. I kept a fake smile plastered to my face throughout, not wanting to spoil Hayden and Astrid's big day.

"What's up buttercup?"

I turned to find Hayden standing behind me. His hair was plastered to his head with sweat, and his face was red with the exertion of dancing all evening.

I wondered if I should tell him about Ari, but then I realized the pounding in my heart had died down. It could have been the champagne I'd consumed, but I didn't think so. Ari had gone.

"Not much. I'm just trying to consume my own weight in alcohol. Are you having a good time? It looks like Astrid has worn you out." I looked up at the dance floor to see Astrid dancing with Hayden's father. They both looked to be having a great time.

"It's been a great wedding. Thanks for being my best man."

"Anytime." I grinned at him. "Who would have thought we'd end up here?"

"So I have a question." Hayden began.

"If you've come to me to ask for advice about what to do on your wedding night, you've picked the wrong best man!" I said, following it up with a hiccup.

Hayden playfully punched my arm lightly.

"Idiot! I was actually wondering how you know Joshua Davenport?"

"Who?" I screwed up my eyes. The alcohol was really beginning to affect me now. Whatever I'd said to Hayden about consuming staggering amounts of the stuff, the truth was, I'd only had two glasses. My own and the glass my mother had left behind. I was such a lightweight that those two glasses had made me feel quite tipsy.

"Joshua Davenport, the famous magical archaeologist. I didn't invite him, and Astrid doesn't even know who he is. As you were dancing with the guy, I figured you must have invited him."

"Oh, you mean Josh?" I rolled my eyes and made sure he wasn't within earshot. I saw him in the far corner of the room deep in discussion with Astrid's mother and a couple of her friends. "My mother invited him. She wanted me to have a blind date with him, but he annoyed the hell out of me."

I saw Hayden raise a brow. "You make me laugh. Every woman in the whole of the kingdom...no, make that the whole nine kingdoms is after him."

I looked over at him again. Astrid's mother did seem rather enamored by him, and the number of women circling him was growing by the minute.

He caught my eye and winked again. Goodness me, he was infuriating. At least he hadn't lied to me like I thought he had. He really was a magical adventurer.

"How do you know of him?" I asked Hayden, turning back to face him so I wouldn't have to look at Josh anymore.

"How do you not know of him? He's on TV all the time. I love his show, *Josh's Journeys into the Unknown*.

"I don't have time to watch TV. I'm the monarch remember?"

Hayden laughed. "No, you aren't. Not officially yet anyway. About that. Do you have a set date for the coronation yet?"

I sighed loudly. The coronation was becoming a thorn in my side. Everything that could go wrong had gone wrong. "Not yet. I keep getting given dates, and then something happens, and the date gets put back. It will be the next century at this rate... Is Josh magic himself?"

No one in Trifork had magic, at least, none of the people native to Trifork. The merpeople had some magic, with my grandfather being the most powerful now that the sea witch was gone, but even then, he couldn't perform most spells. The merfolk had a special kind of magic that was less waving magic wands and more about helping people be able to breathe underwater. My grandfather could do a little more than that, but on the scale of magical beings, he was close to the bottom.

I hadn't met many magical folk. I'd met the queen of Silverwood's husband who was a mage plus a few other dignitaries from other lands who knew magic, but I'd never actually seen any performed.

"He's from Schnee, which is one of the most magically powerful of the nine kingdoms, but his magic is being able to work with magical artifacts. He uses them to perform the magic. I think without them- he's no more powerful than you or I, but he's got the guts of a lion. You should have seen some of the things he's done."

"Fighting a dragon?" I ventured.

"In one episode he did. The dragon burned most of his hair off. He had to do the rest of the season with a half bald head."

I sputtered the sip of champagne I'd just taken, drenching the table in front of me in a very unladylike manner. The image of Josh with half a bald head struck me as funny. Maybe I'd just drunk too much champagne.

Eventually, the wedding came to a close, and the ship was sailed back to the shore. Astrid and Hayden went up on deck to wave to the media as I went to wake my mother.

She looked so peaceful and yet deathly pale lying on the bed. As I moved to wake her, she shuffled and opened her eyes. Eyes that were unfocused, it was almost as if she didn't know who I was.

"It's time to go." I helped her up as she gazed around the room, looking disorientated. Finally, her eyes came to rest on me. "Is the wedding over?"

I heaved a sigh of relief as she began to look like her old self again.

"Yes. We are coming into dock and Hayden and Astrid are up on deck waving to the media."

"Whatever are they doing that for? The media is only out because you are here. It's not like either of those two is famous."

Yep, my mother was back in spirit too. She kinda did have a point. Before the fake wedding between Hayden and I a few months ago, no one had ever heard of Hayden and Astrid. Since then, though, they'd become famous in their own right. At first, Astrid was cast as the villain in the collective mind of the media, but after a great number of interviews in which I'd assured the people of Trifork that Astrid hadn't stolen Hayden from me, the tide turned, and the public began to love them.

We got snapped too as we left the ship, but I was too keen to get my mother home to hang around. By the time I got her back to the palace, she was beginning to look sleepy again, and I began to think that maybe she hadn't drunk as much as I thought she had and it was actually flu instead. She certainly looked too ill for it to be something as mundane as being drunk. Besides, I'd seen her drunk before, and she didn't look like this. She also kept her alcohol drinking to a minimum in public situations, not wanting to appear anything less than graceful.

One of the servants helped me get her to her room, where she fell onto the bed with her eyes closed.

"Can you ask Lucy to come up here and take a look at her?" I asked the servant while looking down at my comatose mother.

He nodded and left the room.

My mother's breathing was even as if she was sound asleep. Maybe that was all it was, and I was making a fuss out of nothing. I pulled a blanket over her and retreated to my room to get out of the long dress I'd been wearing all day. I pulled on my pajamas and in a fit of curiosity, turned the small TV that sat in the corner of my room on. I flicked through the channels looking for the program that Hayden had mentioned featuring Josh, but he wasn't on. I turned it off feeling pretty stupid and headed out onto the balcony to gaze out at the sea. I'd spent all my life doing that, but it was only recently I'd been more interested in what was underneath it.

Following the habit I'd fallen into, I let my eyes come to rest on the moonlit surface of the water, following the line of silver light down to the rocks. My heart gave a flip when I saw the outline of Ari down there. He was sitting in the place I always met him, waiting for me.

I'd not gone to him earlier, choosing to ignore him instead, but it was clear he wasn't going to stop until I spoke to him. I picked up my dressing gown from my bed and strode purposefully out of my room. I'd cried enough tears over him. It was about time he gave me his side of the story. I wanted to look him in the eyes when he told me about the other girl. Anger coursed through me as I left the palace. Anger that I should have been feeling for weeks, but hadn't been because I'd been spending my time feeling sorry for myself instead.

It was a calm night with a slight breeze. The moonlight made it easier to cross the rocks to get to him. In the distance, to my left, I could see the lights still burning on the ship I'd been on earlier. As a wedding gift, I'd loaned it to Astrid and Hayden so they could go on their honeymoon in it. The plan was for them to spend the night in dock and then set sail at some point tomorrow. They had no set plans. They were just going to sail aimlessly for two weeks, stopping when and where the mood took them. I was envious of their freedom and the fact they were now going to do the very same thing Ari and I had planned to do.

"Erica." A voice took me away from my thoughts. It was coming from the direction of Ari, but it wasn't Ari. Screwing up my eyes, I looked harder at the man on the rocks. The man I'd thought was Ari. It wasn't Ari at all. It was my grandfather.

Disappointment flooded through me, followed closely by fear. My grandfather had no reason to visit me in the middle of the night and even less reason to hide out here by the rocks without coming up to the palace. The servants and guards of the palace all knew him by now and would have helped him up to the palace. He had no reason to be here, not unless there was something wrong.

I scrambled over to him as quickly as I could, trying not to let the disappointment over it not being Ari show.

"What is it, Grandfather? What's the matter?"

Even in the pale blue moonlight, I could see that he was pale, and it was hardly like he had a lot of color to begin with.

"I have an apology to make to you," he wheezed. Something was clearly wrong with him. "I didn't think that it was possible that the sea witch could kill your father from the grave. I still believe that your father died of natural causes, but I shouldn't have been so quick to dismiss the idea. Everyone in Havfrue who dealt with her is now sick. It is no coincidence.

I looked at the grayness of his skin, the black circles under his eyes. He looked exactly like my mother had when I left her in her bedroom. She hadn't drunk too much at all. She was really ill.

"What did the sea witch do for you?" I asked him. I think he knew there was no point trying to hide it. He looked dreadful.

"When I was very young, there was no king or queen in Havfrue. You've seen yourself it is not really much more than a city. Officially, we come under the jurisdiction of Trifork, but back then, no one on land even knew of our existence beyond myth and legend. We were safe from the humans, but between ourselves, we fought. There was no leadership. I went to the sea witch and asked her to help make me king. She was a lot younger then, and it was before she got greedy. She helped, but it came at a price. It always did with her.

"She spent the next fifty years interfering. The stronger her magic became, the more annoying she got. A few years after I'd asked for her help, she decided she wanted to rule instead. I think she was annoyed with herself that she'd helped me come to power. She never let me forget it. As you know, I have some magic myself and was able to keep her mostly happy, but I think this sickness is her revenge."

"What can we do? No one in Trifork knows magic. The closest kingdom to us with magic is Thalia, and that's hundreds of miles away. I doubt they'd help us anyway. Why would they?"

My grandfather slumped even lower. He wasn't quite as sick as my mother looked, but he was heading that way.

"You are the queen. Can't you send some of your men to Thalia and bring someone back to help us? My magic isn't strong enough."

I thought back to the last time I'd seen the king and queen of Thalia. They'd come to my fake wedding with Hayden. I couldn't even remember their names or what they looked like. They were only invited as a courtesy. It was hardly as though we had strong ties with them. I couldn't even remember exactly what magic they had. Looking down at my grandfather's drawn face and thinking of my mother upstairs, I knew I had to do something.

"Can you meet me back here first thing tomorrow? I'll see what I can do."

A Quest

Back in the palace, I quickly found a guard and asked him to get one of the palace drivers to get a car ready for me. Without waiting for a response, I rushed upstairs and grabbed my dressing gown from my room. Back downstairs, the car was already waiting on the front driveway. I could hear its engine turning over as I ran through the entrance hall in my bare feet.

"I'm going out," I shouted to the guard on the door as I raced past him. He must have thought it incredibly odd that I was leaving in my pajamas, but I knew that time was of the essence, and I didn't want to waste it by getting dressed.

"To the dock!" I blurted to the driver. Thankfully, the press was not at the front gate as they usually were when something was happening. They probably were all busy, sorting through the photos they'd managed to get of the

The ship was still in dock as I expected it to be. Hayden and Astrid weren't due to leave for their honeymoon until the next day. My concern was that only Hayden, Astrid, and the crew were left on board and it wasn't them I needed to see.

To my dismay, the gangplank was already up. All the guests must have left the ship already which meant that Josh had left too. I had no idea where to begin to look for him. As he wasn't from Trifork, I assumed he must have been in one of the many hotels, but it would have taken me all night to go around to them all.

Just then I heard a giggle, and someone called my name. I turned to see Astrid's parents getting into a car. "Erica, darling. I thought you'd gone home hours ago. We are just heading home ourselves, do you want a lift?"

I ran over to her, not wanting to shout. Although I couldn't see any, there were bound to be some reporters lurking, and the last thing I needed was for them to hear who I was looking for.

"Actually, I was wondering if you knew where Joshua Davenport is staying?"

"Oh, yes?" she answered, clearly misunderstanding my reasons for wanting to see him. "If I was twenty years younger..." she added dreamily.

"Huh, thirty's more like it," replied Astrid's father gruffly. "Will you get in the car?"

"I don't know, darling, but he told me he was planning to have a gamble at the Trifork Casino. Maybe you'll catch him there."

"Thank you!" I kissed her cheek hurriedly and rushed back to the car.

"To the Casino."

I saw the driver raise his eyebrows in the rear view mirror, but he didn't question me. My only problem now was how I was going to get into one of Trifork's liveliest nightspots in my pajamas without being seen.

The car pulled up outside the huge golden doors of the casino. The building was almost as magnificent as the palace, albeit on a much smaller scale. I hopped out of the car and pulled the hood of my dressing gown over my head after instructing the driver to wait around the back.

The bouncer at the door immediately stopped me. Of course, he did. The Trifork Casino had a strict dress code which I was sure didn't include nightwear.

"I need to get inside," I whispered up to the huge man blocking my entrance. "I'm looking for someone. It's urgent."

"I don't care if you are looking for the queen herself, you can't go in dressed like that. May I suggest one of the gaming establishments on the other side of town? They may be more your speed."

I pulled my hood back a little and stepped into the light. "I am the queen herself!"

His face dropped as he realized what he'd said to me. He immediately dropped to his knees and bowed his head. "I'm so sorry Your Majesty."

A couple of people walking past looked our way. "Please get up. It's ok," I said quickly, aware that we were making a scene.

"I need to get inside. It's urgent. There is someone I really need to speak to."

The burly guard nodded his head in confusion. I guess having the ruler of the kingdom turn up in the middle of the night in her pajamas wasn't in the bouncer manual.

"With all due respect ma'am, if you go in like that, the whole of Trifork society will see you. Can I assume that you don't wish to be seen?"

"No, I don't want to be seen, but this is an emergency."

"Right," He nodded beckoning me to a much smaller less grand door about twenty meters to the right of the glitzy entrance. "This is the staff entrance. Follow me."

I followed him into a grey corridor. It looked nothing like the interior of the casino I'd seen through the large golden doors of the main entrance, but at least, there was no one else around. He took me to a small room with a number of cheap tables and chairs in it. In the corner, were a number of vending machines.

"Who do you need to see? Can you describe them to me?"

I thought about Josh's face, his hair, and his unmistakable cool gray eyes, but then I remembered what Hayden said about him being famous.

"Do you know Joshua Davenport?"

The bouncer wiped his forehead, which was pouring with sweat. Being in this position was making him nervous.

"The TV adventurer guy? Yeah. He's inside. I'll get him for you. Would you like me to tell him that it's you who is looking for him?"

"Yes, please." No point in not telling him. He was going to see soon enough.

I waited for five minutes, feeling more and more frustrated with each passing moment. The tipsiness I'd experienced earlier had now faded, only to be replaced with a dull ache around my temples. I yawned, closing my eyes. I felt so utterly tired. The day felt like it had gone on forever, and by the looks of things, I still had a long time to go until bedtime.

I glanced up at the small plastic clock on the wall which told me that it was actually the next day already. Midnight had passed over two hours ago. No wonder I was tired. I was just wondering if it was possible to get a few minutes napping in by resting my head on the table when Josh walked in. He had a huge smile on his face as he saw what I was wearing.

"Well, well, well, I wasn't expecting to see your nightwear on our first date, but I'll take it."

The bouncer who had led him down here left us alone.

"Do you know how unbelievably rude you are, or are you completely oblivious?" I wondered aloud.

"Hey, I'm only saying what I see. You are the one who turned up at the casino asking to speak to me dressed in little more than her undies."

"I'm the queen of the kingdom!" I retorted huffily.

"Do you want me to bow again? I think I'm getting good at it!"

I stifled the urge to wring his neck. There were much more important things to discuss, and killing him probably wouldn't help beyond making me feel any better.

"You know magic, right?" I asked outright. He sat back in his chair and rested his hands on the table between us.

"Nope."

"Nope?" I asked. "I was told you are famous for it. You said yourself that you were magic."

He twiddled his thumbs. "I know a lot about magic. I can use magic if I find a magical object. Without such an object I can't do diddly squat. Don't tell anyone that, though. I like to maintain an air of mystery for my adoring fans."

"How on earth do women fall over themselves for you?" I asked him, completely going off topic.

"My rugged charm," he grinned back at me.

I took a deep breath, remembering why I was here and how urgent it was.

"I need your help..."

"So you didn't come here to seduce me?"

"No! I most certainly did not!" I wrung my hands together.

"Members of my family are ill. A lot of people are ill, and I think it's some kind of magical curse or spell. The problem I have is that the person that cast the spell has been dead for months and no one in Trifork has the ability to reverse it. Do you know anything about magic like that?"

He put one of his hands up to his chin and stroked his none existent beard.

"That's an interesting one, Queenie. You've caught my attention. Carry on."

"I've already told you everything," I replied, trying to keep my temper under control and not admonish him for calling me Queenie.

He gazed at me, leaving an uncomfortable silence between us.

"What?" I asked, breaking the silence.

"No one in Trifork knows magic. I know everything about every magical being in the nine kingdoms, and, therefore, I know you are holding something back."

I rolled my eyes. "For someone who professes to know everything, you are awfully ignorant. Don't you read the papers?"

"Not really"

"My grandfather is a merman. The woman who put the spell on the people who are now sick was a sea witch."

"Your grandfather is a merman?" He sat forward, and for the first time, he looked genuinely interested. His eyes lit up with excitement.

"You are a quarter mermaid? Wow," He exhaled sharply.

"Half, actually. My mother is a full mermaid. The sea witch gave her legs when she was younger, and she's lived on land ever since."

"In all my travels, I've come across a great many beings that most people think are a myth, but I've yet to meet a mermaid."

He looked at me much more closely, his eyes heading southwards to my pajama bottoms.

I don't have a tail," I said, pulling my legs under my chair. Do you think you can help me? If you don't know magic yourself, do you know anyone who does? The closest kingdom I can think of that might be able to help is Thalia.

He shook his head. "The people of Thalia won't be able to help you. Not in this case. They do know magic, but if the legends of the merpeople are true, land magic won't help. I'm guessing this sea witch wasn't a mermaid? Merfolk don't have the magical ability to cast spells that hang around after death. No, she was something much more powerful."

I shook my head, remembering the old hag. It was hard to say what she was. She had tentacles for legs and stole body parts from other people.

"Did she look odd? Can you describe her?"

"She was old-looking although she had patches of new skin. She almost looked like a patchwork quilt. Most of her body didn't even belong to her. She stole my friend's blonde hair. You saw that yourself. Astrid didn't start out with green hair."

"Yes!" Josh stood up and banged his fist on the table. "I knew it! I knew they existed." He spun around on the spot, caught up in his own little world.

"Knew what existed?"

"She wasn't a sea witch, she was a beauty siren."

I raised my eyebrows so high they must have almost touched my hairline.

"I don't know what a beauty siren is, but there is no way in this world that she was one. She was the strangest, ugliest...thing I've ever laid my eyes on. There is no way you could describe her as beautiful."

Josh sat down again and leaned right across the table.

"No, but the way you described her sounds just like these creatures who are fabled to live in distant lands across the ocean. There has been the odd story of sailors lured to their deaths on the rocks near a small group of islands about five hundred miles south of here. Legend has it that they stay young by taking the body parts of the sailors and craft them into new body parts for themselves. They are almost indestructible and live for hundreds of years. Many people have set out to find them, and almost none have made it back. I told my bosses at the studios that I wanted to do a series out there, but they wouldn't let me. They didn't believe that beauty sirens existed, and now, I know they do."

Despite what Josh said, I still couldn't picture the sea witch as a beauty siren.

"Ok, say these beauty sirens exist and say we can find them. Will they be able to reverse this sickness?"

He looked thoughtful for a second. "I don't know, but I think they are the best chance we've got. No land magic will be able to help. Not even the magic in Schnee which is the most powerful magic in all the nine kingdoms. If you can get me a boat, I can get the studio execs on board with it. You being queen will boost the ratings for sure."

I rubbed my temples, trying to take everything in. I'd woken up yesterday morning feeling excited about an upcoming wedding, and here I was less than twenty-four hours later planning a trip across the ocean with a guy I'd only just met. A guy that was a raving lunatic with no manners whatsoever to boot. Plus he wanted it all to be televised. I was really beginning to regret drinking the champagne now.

"I need your help, but I'm not appearing on TV. This is important. I'll get one of the kingdom's naval ships and a crew ready for first thing tomorrow morning. I'll meet you at the dock at nine am."

The grin almost split his face as I stood up and shook his hand. I wasn't sure what I was letting myself in for, but I was pretty sure I was going to regret it.

I left him there and headed back to the palace. I was so unbelievably tired, but there was still so much to do. My first job was to wake John. He lived in the palace in one of the larger staff quarters. I almost never walked down the staff wing as it was their private home, and I didn't want to intrude, but he'd understand.

He was bleary-eyed as he opened the door.

"Ma'am, what's the matter?" He asked in concern as he took in my appearance. I hadn't seen my reflection in hours, but I knew I wasn't looking my best.

I explained the situation and asked him to bring one of the naval ships into dock for me.

He was reluctant to let me go, but I assured him I was in good hands. The mention of Josh's name put him at ease. I guess it wasn't just the ladies that fell for Josh's charms.

After everything was done, I fell into bed, but not before setting my alarm clock for seven. It was only a few hours away, but there were things I needed to do before joining Josh on the ship. I closed my eyes and drifted away almost the instant my head hit the pillow. It felt like a lot less than four hours when the blaring of the alarm clock woke me up.

After dragging myself out of bed and checking up on mother, who had been moved to the palace infirmary overnight, I asked a maid to pack me some clothes and then headed out to the ocean. I stripped down to my underwear and dived straight in, expecting my grandfather to be there. He wasn't, so I began the long swim to Havfrue alone, hoping to meet him somewhere along the way.

After swimming for a full half-hour, I was exhausted, and still, my grandfather hadn't shown. It was a clear day, and the sea was calm, but I'd already swum further than I'd ever swum before, and I was exhausted. Without my grandfather's help, I wouldn't be able to dive below. When I was about where Havfrue was, I dived under the ocean, holding my breath.

My eyesight wasn't the best without a merperson holding onto me, but the spire of my grandfather's palace was hard to miss.

I swam back up to the surface and took a few deep breaths, holding my arms and legs out wide so I could float on the surface and conserve the little energy I had left.

There was no way I'd be able to make it back to land now. The only option I had was to hold my breath and hope someone got to me before my lungs imploded.

There was another way. I lay bobbing on the surface looking up to the clouds and wondered if I should call for Ari. He'd hear me for sure. I was definitely close enough, but I knew I wasn't ready to see him, to confront him. Instead, I breathed deeply and evenly for a few minutes and then with one enormous breath, I plunged under the surface of the water and dove down, right into the heart of Trifork. It was one of my mother's sisters that found me. The youngest one whose name was Cordelia. As she grabbed my arm, relief flooded through me as I no longer needed oxygen from the air. She swam with me into the great underwater palace and into the room that used magic to fill it with oxygen. I always felt strange in here as though the atmospheric pressure was somehow wrong, but it was the only way I could speak to the merpeople.

"What are you doing out here?" Cordelia asked, her long red hair now falling limply over her shoulders now that we were no longer in water.

"I came to speak to Grandfather. I told him I'd meet him out at the rocks this morning, but he never came."

Cordelia squeezed my hand. "He's not very well, Erica. He couldn't come to you."

"He told me that the people of Havfrue were getting sick. My mother is sick too. I have the best physicians in the whole of Trifork looking after her, but she's getting worse. I just lost my father. I can't lose her too."

Cordelia was only a few years older than me, but it seemed that she was much older as she took control and pulled me into a hug.

"It's not everyone. Just those that sought out magic from the sea witch."

I pulled back and looked into her eyes. They were green just like my mother's and just like mine.

"Did you know she wasn't a sea witch?"

Cordelia pulled her eyebrows together. "She was as far as I knew. I barely ever saw her. She scared the heck out of me. Besides, after your mother left, my father banned me and my sisters from ever going to see her."

"Have you ever heard of a beauty siren?" I asked. I hoped she'd say yes because if even so much as one other person had heard of them, I'd feel less like I was about to venture out into a wild good chase, but she shook her head.

Why did I have the feeling I'd be wasting my time with a complete moron while my mother and grandfather were getting weaker. Not that I had any choice in the matter. I needed to do something, and I was all out of options.

I could feel the pull of Ari near me, which wasn't helping me keep a clear head and keep my emotions in check. If I didn't get away soon, I was going to start crying again, and there was already enough salt in the ocean without me adding to it.

"Is Ari okay?" I asked. He was one of the last people to have been tricked by the sea witch or beauty siren or whatever she was. If my mother and grandfather were ill, it stood to reason that he'd have the same sickness.

"I don't know. I haven't seen much of him. Do you want me to take you to him?"

I didn't have a watch, but I already knew I was running short on time. Just getting here had taken a whole lot longer than I had thought and if I didn't hurry back to shore, I'd be late in meeting Josh.

"I can't. I'm going on a trip. Someone is taking me to a group of islands where there might be the magic we need to stop this sickness. Please, will you tell Grandfather I'm going to do my best to find the cure?"

"Of course, would you like me to tell Ari the same thing?"

I thought back to Ari with that other girl. She'd be looking after him now. I shook my head. "No, but please can you take me back home? I don't think I have it in me to swim back on my own."

The journey back to the shore was so much quicker than the journey out, but I'd lost so much time. I ran into the palace up to my room where I got dressed in dry clothes and picked up the suitcase that the maid had packed for me. At the door to the entrance hall, I asked the guard to put it in one of the cars and have the car ready for me.

Downstairs, I found John working away in his office. Anthony was right beside him.

"I heard about your little trip," Anthony said when he looked up and saw who had entered the office. "I know Mother is sick, but do you think now is the time to go gallivanting off on some treasure hunt in the weeks before you become queen. The other kingdoms are wondering why Trifork remains without an official ruler and I'm sure some of them smell weakness."

"Trifork isn't a dog, Anthony. This is the only way I know to help Mother."

"She has round the clock care," he said, standing up. "Meanwhile, our trade deals are

135

beginning to fall apart, people on the borders of Eshen are getting tense, and basically, everything is going to shit."

He slammed his fist down hard on John's desk, making everything on it jump up in the air.

I opened my mouth wide. I'd never seen this side of Anthony before. Where was my dorky, nose-picking younger brother? At some point, while I'd been caught up in all my own problems, Anthony had become a man. At sixteen years old, he was already running the kingdom better than I could. I didn't even know about any trade deals.

"It's hardly my fault that Trifork is without a ruler right now. You two are the ones that were supposed to be dealing with the building works at the Minster. I was happy to hold the coronation here, but that wasn't the right way, remember? It seems that you both have everything in hand, so until the time comes when I can actually be the queen, I don't think the kingdom will fall apart if I go and try and save the people of Havfrue."

Anthony rolled his eyes. "You are needed here. Havfrue has its own people to look out for it."

Unlike everyone else at the palace, Anthony had never really accepted his merman roots. He stayed out of the way when our grandfather came to visit and didn't particularly enjoy talking about the sea.

"The point is moot anyway I'm afraid, Erica," John stood, seeing the fight between siblings about to blow up. "All our naval ships are out at sea. I wasn't able to procure one for your mission."

"What is the fastest time we can get one of them back?" I asked, suddenly feeling panicked.

John shook his head sadly. "The nearest one is over a week away."

A week. I had a feeling that my mother, grandfather, Ari, and the rest of the merfolk didn't have a week left.

The Ruined Honeymoon

It was with the heaviest of hearts that I pulled up at the dock. Throughout the short journey, I'd been wracking my brains trying to think of a way to get help to us more quickly. I remembered what Josh had said about Thalian magic being almost useless in this situation, but I didn't see that there was any choice. Some magic was better than none. I'd already decided to send some of my guards over the Thalian border when Josh sauntered up looking strangely chipper for someone who'd spent half the night playing poker or roulette or whatever his particular game was.

"I can't get a ship out to us in time. We can't go." I said it straight out. There was no point beating about the bush.

Josh sucked in his lips and raised his eyes over my head to something behind me.

"What about that one?"

I turned to see what he was looking at. Behind me was the ship I'd brought in for Hayden and Astrid's wedding, and by the look of it, it was about to set sail.

A grin spread across my face. I hadn't been planning to take over their honeymoon, but if I knew Hayden and Astrid like I thought I did, they would relish the chance of an adventure. Just as long as we let them have their own room.

"Hold up!" I shouted to the dock guard who was untethering the ship from the dock. "You have two new passengers."

The gangplank was let down and the ship door opened as I grabbed my bag of clothes from the back of the car.

"Tell John I found a ship," I called over to the driver. "And ask Anthony to send some guards to Thalia to bring a mage back to the palace."

However much I was needed in Trifork, the people of Havfrue needed me more, not to mention my mother. Josh was already on board as I pelted across the dock and jumped across to the ship. Almost as soon as my feet hit the wood of the deck, the ship set sail. Slowly at first, but as soon as we were out of the dock the main sails were let out, and we picked up speed.

"Brilliant!" exclaimed Josh looking out to the wide expanse of blue ahead of us. Early morning sun sparkled, sending glints of light bouncing off the surface of the water. A cool breeze pushed us on our way through the perfect sailing conditions.

"This is what I've been waiting for my whole life!" I cried out, filled with excitement about my first adventure abroad. In my giddy excitement, I hugged Josh, before remembering I didn't like the guy and dropped my arms to my side.

The ship cut through the sea like a warm knife through butter, and as I held onto the rail and watched the shore get smaller and smaller, my heart felt lighter and lighter.

"I'm not topping myself!" I warned Josh as I stepped onto the lower rail and leaned far over the side. The feel of the wind on my face and the smell of the fresh sea air made me feel like I was flying free like a bird.

"Even so, I'd feel safer if I held onto you. I wouldn't want you to accidentally fall overboard."

"I'm a half mermaid. The ocean is my element."

I had no idea why I said that. Up until a few months ago, I could barely swim at all. Still, I guess it sounded impressive. I could tell that Josh was more interested in me now that he knew my heritage and not in the same creepy way he'd been interested before.

I still didn't like the guy, but I had to admit, without him, I'd be sitting by my mother's bedside watching her die and feeling more and more hopeless with each passing second.

"I know we are close, but I wasn't expecting you to join us for a threesome."

I turned around to see Hayden. He had a grin on his face but also a look of curiosity.

I ran to him and gave him a hug.

"Or should I say foursome," he whispered in my ear. I punched him playfully on the arm.

"I'm sorry, Hayden. We'll leave you and Astrid alone, but we needed the ship, and you said yourself that you had no particular destination in mind. Think of us as your tour guides to a strange new world."

He arched his brow. "Come again?"

Just then, Astrid appeared behind Hayden.

"Erica!" she squealed in surprise. "What are you doing here? Oh, and…"

"Joshua Davenport," Josh ambled over to her, took her hand and kissed it, making her giggle. The action elicited a grimace from Hayden that almost made me laugh.

She looked over at me expectantly, and so I told them both in fine detail what we were doing here and why we had to hijack their honeymoon.

"Why doesn't it surprise me that you ended up with us on our honeymoon?" said Hayden, his voice full of laughter. "You just love playing the third wheel, don't you?"

"Shut it, unless you want me to throw you overboard," I retorted.

He held his hands up and grinned.

"I promise that after we've found these beauty siren people and saved the people of Havfrue, you can have the ship to yourselves…unless we end up going to war which we possibly might the way Anthony tells it."

"Do you even know where these islands are?" Hayden asked, his tone changing to something more serious. I probably should have felt more serious about the mission myself, considering half of Havfrue was dying, but I knew we were close to it which meant the bonding had kicked in again. Being bonded to a merman who wanted someone else was awfully inconvenient.

"Not exactly," I admitted.

"I don't have a map, but I know approximately where they are rumored to be," said Josh stepping forward.

"Rumored?"

I took a deep breath, knowing how crazy it sounded as Josh spoke again.

"The islands are legendary and are not plotted on any map, but if you'll permit me to go and speak to the captain, I can give him a general idea as to which course to plot."

"Soooo...." Hayden spoke slowly, and I already knew what was coming. "These islands and these beauty sirens might not exist?"

Josh nodded his head cheerfully as though the actual existence of them was second only to the adventure we were embarking on

Josh was saved having to answer by Astrid chipping in. "Hayden, go and introduce Joshua to the captain. I'll figure out somewhere for these two to sleep."

Just then, I heard someone coughing. We all turned as a man with a long, shaggy beard, and a camera came out of the shadows. It looked like he'd just finished filming us.

Josh walked toward him and clapped him on the back.

"Everyone, this is Seth, my cameraman. He's going to be filming the adventure."

"Filming?" inquired Hayden.

"For my TV show. This is going to be the best series yet."

If looks could kill, Josh would have been double zapped. It seemed Hayden was equally as unimpressed with having a cameraman on board as I was. Astrid, on the other hand, patted her hair and then held her hand out to shake Seth's hand.

I pulled Josh to one side and hissed in his ear. "When did he come aboard?"

Seriously, I'd not taken my eyes off Josh or the ship for one second while we were at the docks. Had Josh stashed him on there before I'd even turned up, knowing I'd say no to having him here?"

Josh shrugged. "While you were getting your bag from the car. Didn't you see him? I told you I was going to film this. This is the adventure of a lifetime. I was hardly going to pass up the chance to share it with my fans."

I stared at him in what I hoped conveyed the message that I was angry. It was difficult as my heart was pounding with my proximity to Ari somewhere below us. "I said I didn't want a cameraman on this ship!"

"What you actually said was that you don't want to appear on TV. You said nothing about the others. I'll ask Seth to keep your airtime to a minimum. I can always have you edited out."

I stared at him, open-mouthed at the sheer balls of the guy as he herded both Hayden and Seth into the ship.

"This is so exciting!" Astrid chirruped as she bounded over to me. "That guy is gorgeous. I saw you dancing with him at the wedding and was wondering who he was. What's with the cameraman? Is he famous? Is he your boyfriend?"

I guess Astrid watched about as much TV as I did.

I rolled my eyes at her. Making sure the boys had gone and were out of earshot.

"No, he is most definitely not my boyfriend although my mother set us up before she got sick. He's an idiot with an ego the size of Trifork, but he knows his stuff...at least I think he does. Put it this way, he's the only chance we have."

"At least, we have a lead," she said, linking her arm in mine. "I'm sorry to hear about the queen...queen mother. How are you feeling? You must be pretty frazzled."

I took a deep breath. Frazzled was one word for it.

"I want to say I feel sad and depressed because I know I should, but I think we are passing over Havfrue and you know what that means. I feel like a butterfly taking flight for the first time. My heart is beating ninety to nothing, and I can't stop smiling. This bonding is maddening."

Astrid looked over my shoulder and frowned. "Erica, look. The shore is almost out of sight. We passed over Havfrue ages ago. Whatever is going on with you has nothing to do with Ari."

I turned back to see for myself. She was right. Havfrue was miles behind.

On Film

"I'm really sorry that we invaded your honeymoon."

"I'm sorry that you have to sleep in here," replied Astrid as she showed me to one of the private quarters. It was small with a set of bunk beds and a small wardrobe for clothes. "Hayden and I have the Captain's quarters, and the captain is in the first officer's quarters which leaves only these small rooms for the higher officers and the dorms for the lower ones. There's not much in the way of privacy I'm afraid."

I looked around the room that would be my home for the next few days. At least, it had a porthole which meant I could watch the world go by in peace. "I love it! Just don't put Josh and Seth near me. They can have one of the dorms on the other side of the ship."

Astrid sat on the lower bunk as I pulled my clothes from my bag and began to hang them up.

"Is he really all that bad?" she asked. "I mean, he's pretty gorgeous."

"Looks aren't everything. Moron is not a strong enough word for him. He's the worst. Stupid, but thinks he's smart. That's a dangerous combination in my books."

Astrid lay back, placing her head on her hands on top of the pillow. "You think he's dangerous? I kinda like that in a man."

"Pffft!" I laughed out loud, taking a seat on the end of the bed by her feet. "I didn't say *he* was dangerous. I'm sure he's pretty harmless, but I'm worried that this whole trip will turn out to be a complete waste of time. I'm worried that someone will die while I'm away chasing myths and legends with some lunatic, and I'll have missed the chance to say goodbye. Everyone speaks highly of him, but I know how television works. Things are not always what they seem. He's probably some dunderheaded pretty boy who fronts the show, and the real brains of the operation is sitting in a leather office chair drinking cocktails somewhere."

I heard a sniff. Turning to look at Astrid, I found her crying. Tears streamed down her face making her skin appear blotchy and her eyes red. I scrambled in my bag for a handkerchief, and when I found it, I passed it to her.

"Sorry, I'm just emotional. You won't miss your chance to say goodbye. Your mom will be fine."

Astrid and my mother hadn't gotten off to the best start but they'd bonded over the wedding planning. I'd not realized how much my mother being sick had affected her.

I should have been crying too. The people I cared about the most in the world were gravely ill, and yet, my insides felt like I was on a thrill ride. Having passed over Havfrue and therefore Ari, my heart rate should have subsided, but I could still feel it pounding away in my chest. For a second I wondered if I were ill too, but then I remembered that no one else had complained of a pounding heart or the immense feeling of true love.

I stood up and helped Astrid to her feet. She silently hugged me, and I was grateful for her friendship. Not many people would let their best friend come on their honeymoon with them, let alone a complete stranger and a cameraman. Astrid was one in a million. I had a feeling Hayden wasn't quite so accepting, but he'd come around. He had told me he was a fan of Josh's TV show after all.

Dinner that evening was an interesting affair. The food was good, thanks to us having a highly trained kitchen staff onboard, but the atmosphere was frosty at best. While Astrid and I had been sorting bunks and gossiping, it seemed that Hayden and Josh had had some serious disagreement when the captain had pointed out that the islands that Josh spoke about didn't exist. Apparently, Josh's comeback had been that just because they weren't on any map, didn't mean they didn't exist.

Astrid chatted with Josh about his TV show while I ended up talking to Hayden. Seth had elected to eat in his bunk, and beyond him popping up here and there with his camera, I'd barely spoken to the guy.

"Do you think this guy is a phony?" Hayden leaned toward me and whispered. I looked over at Josh. He was deep in conversation with Astrid who seemed delighted to be chatting with him. Her face was animated, and every so often she'd give a small peal of laughter at one of his stories. I screwed my face up. I wanted to be able to tell Hayden that I thought Josh was a genius, but Hayden knew me too well for me to let a lie slide by him.

"I have no idea if this will pan out," I replied honestly. "You know the guy better than I do. Don't you watch his TV show?"

"Yeah, but I only know him as the celebrity. I don't know the real him." He let out a breath between clenched teeth, and I could see that he was getting mad. "He's known as a womanizer. Did you know that?"

"Stop it!" I hissed under my breath. "You have no need to be jealous if that's what this is. Astrid loves you. Please don't be an idiot or I'll think the sea witch has put a spell on you again."

As I said it, I realized that it wasn't just the merfolk that had been plagued by the sea witch. Only a few months ago, she'd made Hayden believe he was in love with me. He'd acted like a dolt back then too.

"How are you feeling?" I asked him. He looked at me with a confused expression on his face at the sudden change of subject.

"Fine...why?"

I leaned even further in. I really didn't want Astrid to hear what I was about to say and panic. "Everyone that the sea witch put a spell on has become sick. She put a spell on you too. I'd completely forgotten about it until now."

Hayden shook his head. "I'm honestly fine apart from the fact that my new wife is currently on my honeymoon with a jumped-up pretty boy, and I'm stuck talking to you."

"Thanks!" I replied, my voice dripping in sarcasm.

"I'm sorry. I shouldn't have said that." He placed his hand on my shoulder and gave me a smile. "You know I love you. You are my best friend...I just..."

I stood up, picking up my plate of half-eaten food.

"Josh," I called across the table. "It's a lovely evening. Care to join me on deck?"

I gave Hayden a wink as Josh followed my lead. When I looked back, Hayden mouthed a silent thank you.

Outside, it was actually pretty blustery which made eating more difficult than I imagined. It didn't help that neither of us had thought to bring cutlery with us.

"How am I supposed to eat this?" asked Josh, looking down at his plate.

I shrugged my shoulders. "You are an adventurer; I'm sure you'll figure it out. Here, can you hold this? I'll be right back." I passed my plate to him and slipped back inside. Instead of heading to the dining hall, I turned to the galley. The ship's cook was very happy to fulfill my request that a bottle of the finest champagne be brought to the dining room along with a bucket of ice. The request for candles was denied for safety reasons as the ship was made out of wood, but I figured the champagne would placate Hayden a little.

When I got back on deck, I found Josh eating his steak with his hand. My plate had been placed on the floor. I picked it up and followed his lead.

The sun was beginning to set, and the sea had taken on an orange-pinkish hue. The silence was only cut by the sound of gentle, lapping of the waves below us and the flapping of the sails. This is what I'd waited my entire life for and despite the dire situation back home, I felt incredibly happy. I felt the same as when Ari was near me, but he was so many miles back now. Maybe it was my childhood dream being realized that made me feel the way I did.

"It feels entirely inappropriate," I pointed out, forgetting that Josh didn't know my situation with Ari.

"You and me being together...alone?" He made a step toward me.

"Hold it, Buster!" I held my hand out to stop him coming even closer to me. "I wasn't talking about that. I was talking about how happy I feel despite everyone being sick. I should feel so much worse than I do."

Josh nodded his head thoughtfully and gazed out into the never-ending distance. "It's the ocean. It can do that to a person. Being away from people is my happy place. It doesn't have to be the ocean. I'm just as happy at the top of a mountain or the middle of a jungle. Anywhere where people are scarce or better yet, not there at all."

I thought about it for a moment. I didn't think that's why I was happy. I liked being surrounded by people most of the time. It was the adventure I craved. The ability to be free and to see new things.

I couldn't really understand what was going on inside me. The further away I was from Ari, the worse I should feel, but it was like he was right next to me. Maybe we weren't bonded after all. The whole concept was ridiculous anyway.

"Do you know anything about bonding?" I asked. The guy seemed to know about everything else.

"Bonding? As in two people coming together?" He licked his lips and took a step forward once again, causing me to take a step back.

"You are particularly vile, you know that?"

He held his hands up. "Sorry. Bonding? Like the magic kind?"

I thought for a moment. When Ari had described it to me, he had talked about magic.

"Yes. Specifically in relation to merpeople."

Josh's eyes lit up. It was clear that magic was his favorite subject. "Magical bonding only happens within certain species. Humans think it happens to them, but they call it love at first sight or soul mates. It's all a load of phooey. I've found my soul mate plenty of times only to find out that she was ordinary."

I lifted my lip and nose at the thought of him with all those girls. I had no idea why I'd asked him. The dude obviously had no idea about love.

"Never mind." I turned to go back inside. It was early, but I'd rather be alone in my bunk than hang around with this creep.

"Hey, wait! Are you talking specifically about bonding between merpeople? Because that totally is a thing. At least, I read that it was. Are you bonded to someone?"

I sensed that whatever I told him would end up on TV, so I elected to go with a lie. "No. I just heard about it and was curious."

"Bonding is when two people...in this case, two merpeople are destined to be together. Their love for each other is so strong that it can never be broken. It is love in its most pure base form. It is beauty and truth combined. It is heady and dangerous and beautiful all in one."

He took a step toward me, and this time, I stayed where I was, mesmerized by his speech. I felt my breath catch in my throat as he placed his hand on my cheek, and I found myself looking deeply into those light eyes.

"Those who are bonded will either live a glorious life together or a life of torment if they are forced apart. It is both a blessing and a curse, and for those of us that are purely human, we will never be able to understand the piercing pain nor the uneclipsed high of being bonded. It is said that it is a torture beyond any other and a bliss to which nothing in the nine kingdoms can compare."

He bridged the gap between us, putting his lips upon mine as we leaned against the railing of the ship. I closed my eyes, falling into the kiss, but then, a pain shot through my heart as though an arrow had pierced my skin and traveled right through my ribcage.

I screamed as the searing pain took over, overwhelming my senses. I felt Josh rubbing my back as I bent double in agony. My chest was on fire, and then...and then, it wasn't.

Less than a minute after it had started, the pain ebbed away. I pulled myself up straight and stared down at my chest, looking for a gaping wound or any other clue as to what had just happened to me.

Everything looked normal. I sucked in a deep breath, trying to fight the shock. The pain had vanished, but I knew the memory of it would last a long time.

"Are you alright?" Josh asked concern in his voice.

"I'm fine," I lied. "I think I was stung by a bee, that's all. I should probably go and lie down." I turned to leave him feeling completely confused. Everything had been normal before Josh kissed me and almost as soon as his lips touched mine, it felt as though my insides were exploding. I ran back along the deck. Before I reached the door, I saw the telltale light of a video camera. The whole episode had been captured on film.

The Map

My breathing came thick and fast as I lay on the top bunk of my cabin. The ship swayed lightly from side to side making me feel more nauseous than I already did.

My heart had settled down, back to the state it was in before Josh kissed me. It felt like Ari was close, which made me feel even worse about the whole thing.

I closed my eyes and tried to work out what had happened. I'd been fine until Josh had kissed me. It wasn't like he'd forced himself onto me. I was a willing participant, but that didn't mean I really wanted to do it. Or had I? He was a good-looking guy; there was no doubt about it, but he was also an annoying, egotistical rat. I imagined he had a girl in every port. I could see what girls saw in him, but he wasn't my type at all. I don't even know why I'd let him kiss me. I wasn't attracted to him. My only reasonable conclusion was that it was a heat of the moment thing. He'd been talking about blissful love, and I was a willing captive to his words. Of course, I was. Since Ari, I'd been lonely, fulfilling my duties as the future queen and dealing with crap from all sides. Not only did I have one kingdom to deal with, I was looking after two.

"No wonder I slipped up," I whispered to myself.

Still, it didn't explain what the pain was. It was gone completely, but for the minute I'd been feeling it, it was the most intense agony I'd ever had to bear.

Hayden had told me that Josh was from Schnee. Of all the magic in all of the nine kingdoms, Schnee was the most powerful. I'd have sent some of my guards there to find help for my mother and grandfather had it not been for the fact it was well over a thousand miles away from my palace in Trifork.

The king and queen never accepted any invitation from us, and although I couldn't call them enemies of Trifork, they were hardly allies either. The people from Schnee tended to keep themselves to themselves.

If the people of Schnee were so powerful, why was it that Josh held no magic of his own? He'd said himself he was powerless without magical artifacts. It only cemented my theory that the man was a liar. Everyone in Schnee was magic, so it stood to reason Josh was too.

It still didn't answer the question as to why, if he wanted to kiss me, he'd immediately strike me down with pain. Feeling like your insides are trying to escape to the outside is hardly the most romantic feeling in the world.

It took me hours to fall asleep, and it was a gentle knock at my door that awoke me the next morning.

"Erica, Are you ok? Breakfast is served in the dining hall."

Bleary-eyed, I dragged myself out of bed and opened the door to find Astrid standing there looking perky as usual. I pulled her into my room, making sure there was no one lurking in the corridor, and shut the cabin door behind her.

"What's the matter?" She looked at me in alarm.

I told her what had happened last night and also mentioned that I was still feeling Ari's presence even though he was now hundreds of miles behind us.

She sat me on the lower bunk and looked at me with something akin to pity on her face.

"I wonder if the pain was just a reaction to you moving on. Subconsciously, you still feel as though you are with Ari. I don't know much about bonding, but I imagine it's pretty hard to get over something like that. You probably feel him near you because you don't really want to let him go."

It made sense. The pain was probably a physical manifestation of the guilt I felt at kissing someone else even if it was someone I didn't really want to kiss.

"You are probably right," I sighed. "It's not like it's going to happen again anyway."

Astrid looked at me as though I was crazy. "Why not? The guy is a dish, and you would go together perfectly. You always wanted an adventure and less than a day after meeting him, look where you are!"

"Hmmm," I replied without much conviction. Yeah, I was on an adventure, but that didn't mean I had to date the guy who'd brought me on it.

At the breakfast table, Hayden had a completely different take on the events of the previous night.

In hushed tones, he told me that Josh wasn't to be trusted at all.

"The pain thing is weird. I wonder if he's trying to muscle in, knowing that you are a new queen. It wouldn't surprise me if he's trying to take over in Trifork. Those people from Schnee are very wily and enjoy their power. He might be planning to kill you."

I snorted, sending orange juice flying out of my nose. He was beginning to sound like Anthony with his theories of other kingdoms wanting to take over and Trifork currently being in a weak position without a true monarch yet. After quickly mopping up the juice, I turned back to Hayden.

"You liked him two days ago," I pointed out. As I looked over to the other side of the table, I watched him flirting shamelessly with Astrid who was lapping up all the attention. "You need to stop with this jealousy. The guy is a flirt. Astrid isn't going to leave you for him."

"I never said she would," Hayden answered gruffly, and the conversation ended.

I'd always thought an adventure would be...well, more adventurous, but after the hours and hours of monotony of sailing through calm seas, I had to admit I was getting bored. Bored and fractious. Every second we spent at sea was a second longer that my mother and grandfather and all the others had to wait for help. Even if we found these beauty sirens, there was no telling if they could or would help us. Every time I had a conversation with anyone, Seth always seemed to be there, hiding behind a column or chair or whatever he could find. Nothing was private anymore.

In the end, I decided to head up to the bridge to speak to the captain. He was one of my finest naval officers, after all, and so it was about time I introduced myself to him. My father knew the names of every person who worked for him, both in the palace and on his ships. I, on the other hand, barely remembered my own name when I woke up each day. Remembering names and faces was hardly my strong suit. It was something I had to work on.

The captain and first officer both bowed to me as I entered the bridge. I was surprised to find that the captain was a woman, a young woman at that.

"We heard we had a special guest on board, Your Highness," the captain said, following up the bow with a salute. "I hope you are finding everything to your satisfaction."

"Very much so, Captain..?"

"Captain Howell."

She was so young to be a captain, only twenty-eight or nine with a fresh face free of make-up and her auburn hair tied neatly behind her. Her captain's hat was laid to the side of the ship's steering wheel.

"Captain Howell, I appreciate you doing this for me." I walked to the windows and looked down at the deck to see if I could spot Seth. I didn't want him filming me or even seeing where I was and passing the information back to Josh. The deck was empty, so the pair of them must have been indoors or to the rear of the ship. "I was wondering how much longer it will be until we get to the islands."

Captain Howell looked a little nervous upon hearing my question. "I've sifted through every map I have on board, and those islands aren't on any of them. At the moment, I'm following this..."

She pointed to a crumpled piece of paper with a badly hand- drawn map on it.

"Let me guess. Joshua gave this to you?"

The captain nodded slowly. "Yes, ma'am. I was told by Mr. Harrington-Blythe that I was to follow these instructions, but I had the feeling he wasn't particularly happy about it. Do you have another route for me to follow?"

I looked back at the map. It was ridiculously simple with no coordinates on it, just some squiggly lines and a couple of place names. I sighed wondering what I'd gotten us all into. Either Josh was indeed the simpleton I took him for, and these islands were a figment of his overactive imagination, or he was, as Hayden suspected, dangerous and had brought us out here for his own agenda. My father would have come up with a plan straight away and would have stuck to it with a strong conviction. I wasn't sure what we should do. Carry on with this trip which would probably turn into a wild goose chase and a font of bad publicity if people actually began to die while their queen was out at sea, or turn and head home.

Weighing up the options, neither seemed like a good prospect. But by going home now, we would definitely have nothing to show for this trip. At least, if we kept on going, there was the possibility of finding help.

"If the map is accurate, judging by the places on it that you know to exist, how long do you think it will take?"

Captain Howell looked back at the map and sucked in a breath between her teeth. "It's hard to say, but maybe this afternoon?"

She didn't sound so sure, but then how could I blame her. The map looked like a kid had drawn it.

"Let's keep going on this course until this afternoon and reassess then. Thank you for everything you are doing, Captain. It is very much appreciated."

I spent the rest of the day trying to hide from Josh. I was still confused by what had happened the night before and wasn't sure whether Astrid was right, and my pain had been due to emotional pain or if Hayden was right, and Josh was out to kill me.

Ok, Perhaps Hayden's theory was a tad overdramatic, but I hadn't felt the pain since Josh kissed me. I was still feeling the high I felt when Ari was around.

I was doing a good job of not seeing Josh by hiding in my bunk and reading a book when Hayden knocked on my door and then opened it without giving me a chance to answer.

"Hey! Where are your manners? I could have been changing!"

"I'm sure you've got nothing I haven't seen before. You've got to help me.

"You are so rude! Honestly, I could have you beheaded for less." I stepped down from my bunk, leaving the book on the pillow.

"Please come and talk to Josh. He's driving me crazy. This is supposed to be my honeymoon, and I've spent most of it watching Astrid staring at him all googly-eyed over his ridiculous stories."

I rolled my eyes at him. "Give your wife some credit, will you? I'm sure she wasn't googly-eyed as you put it. She's probably just being polite."

Hayden scoffed as I continued. "But, you are right. This is your honeymoon, and we've hijacked it. Where are they? I'll take Josh for a walk around the decks and ask the kitchen to send our dinner up to the front deck later so you and Astrid can dine alone."

"Bow."

I looked at him through screwed up eyes. "You bow to me. I'm the one who is royal."

He was just about to call me an idiot when I broke out into a grin. "I know the front of a ship is called a bow. Come on, let's go. You have some honeymooning to do."

"Too right, I do," he replied, following me out of my cabin.

Lured

When I found Josh, he wasn't with Astrid at all. I found him standing alone, gazing off into the distance at the bow of the ship. I looked out at the endless sea stretching out for miles ahead of us. There was no sign of land in any direction. Captain Howell said we'd see the islands by the afternoon, but the sky was already beginning to lose color, and there was no sign of them.

"I've asked the chef to have our dinner brought up here," I said, sidling in next to Josh.

He didn't look to me. Instead, he kept his eyes on the horizon.

"Nice...romantic."

"No, not romantic, just nice." I turned so my back was to the rail and glanced around the deck for the telltale red light that showed that

Seth's camera was filming. Thankfully, he was nowhere to be seen. "About last night,, the kiss...I'm sorry, but it shouldn't have happened. I don't know what came over me."

"You couldn't resist my charm." He turned to me and wiggled his eyebrows. I resisted the urge to throw up over the side.

I shook my head. "Nope. I think it was the alcohol I consumed at dinner."

That was a lie, and we both knew it. I'd only had a small glass of wine. The truth was, I didn't know what had come over me.

"You can tell yourself that you aren't attracted to me all you like, but that doesn't make it so."

I pulled on his sleeve so he had to turn to look at me. "The kiss we shared made me physically sick. Please get over yourself."

The corners of his mouth turned up at the edges. "Say what you like, Queenie, but no one has managed to escape the charms of Josh Davenport. By the end of this trip, you'll be begging me to kiss you again."

I scrunched my nose up at him. "You must have a strong neck to carry that big head of yours around."

"Just wait and see." He turned back and returned his gaze to where it had been before. I followed his line of sight to the horizon.

"I thought we'd be at the islands by now," I commented. "The captain seemed to think we'd be there before nightfall, going by your sketch."

"That was no sketch. I gave her a carefully plotted out map using every bit of knowledge I had about those islands."

I thought back to the sketch I'd seen. It certainly didn't look like it was carefully plotted out. Once again, I began to wonder if I was following the directions of a man full of bullshit. So maybe he was a famous adventurer on TV. It didn't mean any of it was real. The bit of TV I knew about was always carefully orchestrated in the edits afterward. For all I knew, Josh spent all his time in front of a green screen and never left the studio.

"Tell me about Schnee. What made you leave?"

The one thing I was pretty confident about him not lying about was his home kingdom. He certainly wasn't from Trifork and had the look about him of a person from Schnee. He had the paleness that I associated with people from there.

"Magic," he replied simply and then stopped. It was unusual for him to not have a lot to say on a subject which made me all the more intrigued.

"What about it?"

Josh closed his eyes and sighed as though this was a topic he really didn't want to talk about. Eventually, he did begin to tell me, although he spoke slowly as though getting the words out was difficult. "Everyone in Schnee is magic, or at least most of the population is. Most people have what you'd think as general magic. They point to objects and make them move, or they conjure things out of mid-air. The royals are the most powerful, but even the lowliest can perform some kind of magic if they have to."

I thought back to what I knew of Josh. Both he and Hayden had told me that he held no real magic power of his own.

"But you can't?"

His eyes misted over, and I began to wonder if I'd pushed the guy too far. This was the first bit of real emotion I'd ever seen from him. Up until now, everything about him had seemed fake.

"I've gotta go...do something. I'll be back for dinner."

He turned away from me and quickly headed for the door inside. I'd promised Hayden that we'd leave him and Astrid alone, but I had a feeling Josh would go somewhere to be alone.

How strange that talk of magic would affect him so. Apparently, he talked about it all the time on his show. It was that which had made him famous.

As I was unable, or at least, unwilling to join Hayden and Astrid, and I didn't fancy going back to my room, I decided to stay outside and enjoy the early evening by myself. The last embers of sunshine turned the sky a dusky pink and the sea an endless expanse of deep mauve, colored by the dying orb of the sun and hiding its mysteries beneath.

This...all of this was the reason I'd wanted adventure. I wanted to feel the thrill of the wind in my hair as we flew through the waves at high speed, but I wasn't enjoying it. We should have hit land by now, and there was no hint of it on the horizon. Josh was upset with me, Hayden didn't want me around, not that I could blame him, and I had no desire to speak to the ever elusive Seth who seemed happiest hiding out and not talking to anyone. Even the bonding feeling—the weird happiness that had plagued me the entire journey was finally beginning to seep away. Maybe I was finally far enough away from Havfrue and, therefore, Ari to not feel him anymore. I let my mind wander to him as it frequently did, before trying to push him out of my mind. There was no point getting myself all miserable again.

A sound behind me made me turn, but it just turned out to be the kitchen staff bringing out a small table and a couple of chairs. They followed it up with a meal of salmon and potatoes with some kind of white sauce. I deliberated going to fetch Josh, but moments later he appeared sitting in the seat opposite me.

He looked back to his normal self, and any hint of whatever had bothered him earlier was now gone.

"Will Seth be joining us?" I asked for want of anything else to say. I didn't want to upset him again by getting back into the whole magic business.

Josh speared a piece of salmon and dipped it in the sauce before replying. "I think he's eating in his room."

I nodded. At least, he wasn't bugging Hayden and Astrid. The dinner was surprisingly quiet. I didn't know what to say, and Josh, it seemed, was finally out of words.

All in all, it was extremely awkward for both of us, and I began to wish that I'd decided to eat in my cabin too. By the time we'd finished our dessert, the sky was pitch black, and only the moon and the stars provided any kind of illumination. We'd also not said another word to each other.

I stood, ready to retire for the evening when I heard the strangest of sounds, almost like singing, but much more eerie. A choir of hauntingly beautiful voices filled the night air all around us, and yet, it sounded as though someone was singing under water. When I'd heard the merpeople speaking, the strange echoing sounds they made sounded a little similar.

The ship lurched as we quickly changed course, sending our dirty plates crashing to the ground where they smashed into tiny pieces.

I jumped up, eager to find out what was making the noise, but Josh held me back.

"It's them!" He rushed to the rail and peered over. In the darkness, it was difficult to see anything, but as the moon came out from behind a cloud, their silhouettes appeared. Beautiful women sitting on rocks. Rocks that if we didn't change course, we were going to crash into.

"Captain Howell!" I screamed, hoping she could hear me up in the bridge. The ship continued on its perilous path.

Josh appeared completely transfixed by the women who were now beckoning him toward them. The moon picked off sparkles of light in their silvery hair—hair that I wanted to touch. It looked so soft and shiny. I reached out over the railing. There was something about them, something mesmerizing that took us ever onward. In the back of my brain, I knew that if we continued on our path, we would crash straight into the rocks, but the rest of me didn't care. It would be a small price to pay to be near these wondrous creatures.

Suddenly, there was a massive splash of water in front of them, knocking them all into the sea. The melodic music cut off, and the spell was broken. My heart that had been strangely calm now began the rapid staccato.

"We need to get this ship turned around quickly!" I cried, but before I'd even finished the sentence, the ship lurched again turning away from the jagged rocks and missing them by inches. The rapid movement knocked me over and sent me skidding across the floor.

"I guess now we know why almost no one made it back from here to tell the tale," Josh said, holding his hand out and helping me to my feet. I glanced over the side of the ship. Hundreds of wrecked boats littered the coast of the strange island leaving a graveyard of sorts.

"I've dropped anchor for the night, ma'am."

I turned to find Captain Howell looking slightly stunned as she gave me a salute.

"They were using magic to lure us onto the rocks," I pointed out. Relief shone from her face as she let out a long breath.

"They sure did! I've never seen anything like it." Josh danced around like he'd just won a party bag or something. "I need to find Seth and see if he captured this." He began to walk away, but I called after him.

"What if they try to kill us some other way in the night? You're the expert. What should we do?"

"They won't," he assured me before practically skipping to the door and heading inside. "They'll leave us well alone."

As I looked over the side to the black water beneath us, an eerie feeling passed through me. The sirens had completely disappeared under the inky surface, but what was it that had startled them in the first place?

As I walked back to my cabin, my heart still pounding, I tried to keep in mind what Josh had said. He'd sounded pretty confident that they wouldn't try and hurt us.

Before the dawn, I was to find out just how wrong he could be.

Sirens

"Come with me."

An ethereal voice woke me from my slumber. As I drifted from my dreams, I came face to face with one of the sirens. Up close, she was even more beautiful than she had been on the rocks. Her title of beauty siren suited her well. She had perfect skin that looked like it had been dusted in fairy dust and her long hair had strands of real silver that glimmered in the pale light. She wore a powder blue dress, the exact same color as her eyes, although the light in her eyes could have been a real diamond, they sparkled so much.

"Come with me," she repeated, not raising her voice. It was melodic and calming—the voice of an angel, and an angel is what she looked like with white feathered wings that she used to keep her upright as she had no legs, only a tail like a mermaid.

"You'd like that wouldn't you?" she added, a smile on her perfect lips.

"I would," I replied groggily. In my mind, I wasn't sure if I was doing the right thing. Everything was hazy. I had the feeling that I was doing something I shouldn't be doing, but the lilting tone of her voice lured me on.

It was almost a dreamlike trance that carried me out of my cabin and through the ship to the deck. Beside me, I was aware of other people congregating, but I couldn't take my eyes off the siren in front of me. She was everything that was perfect and beautiful in the world, and nothing else could compare. Why would I want to look at anything else?

"Take my hand." She held her hand out to me, and I did as she directed. One sharp tug later and we were both in the ocean. She'd pulled me right over the railing, and I didn't even mind. I would go anywhere with her. Unlike when I was with the merfolk, I couldn't breathe underwater. Not that it mattered. I was only submerged for a few seconds, and when I surfaced, I found myself in a strange room. The half I was in was filled with water, the other half had rocks on the floor. Upon these rocks sat more of the divine creatures, at least fifty of them, each more beautiful than the last. One of them ran over to help me out of the water. The creatures were all divine, but none looked like the others. Some had wings, some tails, some legs. All of them had the long silvery hair and diamond-like eyes.

"Let me help you," she said graciously. She waved her hand and instantly I was warm and dry. I was given a seat on the rocks while I waited for the others to join us. Less than a minute after I'd entered the strange room, everyone from the ship had arrived. Josh, Seth, Astrid, Hayden, and the crew. I gave them each a brief nod as they entered, but it was difficult to take my eyes from the women that surrounded us. I managed to steal my eyes away for a second to take in the room around me. The high, vaulted ceiling had a couple of chandeliers hanging, and it was these that gave the room a warm flickering light. Portholes around the walls gave me a clue to what the room actually was.

"It's a boat!" I shouted out in delight, "an upside-down boat!"

"You are very intelligent," one of the women said, taking a handful of my hair in her hands, "and what beautiful hair you have."

My heart swelled with pride at getting a compliment from these women. They were the most beautiful creatures I'd ever seen, and here they were saying they liked my hair. I beamed from ear to ear.

Erica, this isn't real! I heard a voice say, but it didn't come from one of the sirens, so I ignored it.

The siren who had brought me to this place climbed up onto a rock and spoke to all of us.

"Welcome to our home, esteemed guests. My sisters are going to hand out handcuffs which we have chosen specially. When you receive them, you will put them on your wrists and close them tight. It is nearly dawn, and so I'm afraid we must leave you. We will be back tonight with knives for you to cut yourselves with. We need your body parts."

"They are so beautiful," the one next to me said, stroking my skin. I giggled with excitement. The handcuffs seemed to take forever to get to me, and I was practically bouncing up and down with anticipation of putting them on.

Once we were all chained together and to the rocks, the sirens began to leave.

"Where are you going?" I asked in a panic. I knew I couldn't get through a second without them near me. The leader walked over and kissed me lightly on the lips. "Fear not, we will be back, and then this evening, you and I will be joined for the rest of our lives."

The thought of being joined to her was almost too much to bear. How could someone as lowly as I ever be one of these beauties?

"This is the most amazing thing that has ever happened to me," Astrid said in a breathy voice once the sirens had left. The others nodded in agreement, each with a sappy expression on their face. They looked ridiculous. It was obvious that the sirens liked me the best. Hadn't one of them kissed me after all?

"They want me. I was kissed," I pointed out. "It's my body they want, and I shall give it gladly."

"They kissed all of us, you idiot," the captain screamed at me. "I'll give them anything they want. My body is their body."

"I cannot wait to hand them my flesh," added Seth.

Huh. As if they'd want that lump.

"Erica, please snap out of it. You're under a spell."

I felt the cold slap of a palm across my face. In front of me was a man with long black hair and a concerned expression on his face. At the back of my mind, I vaguely recognized him, but he was part of my past, and my future belonged with the sirens.

"Don't mess with my skin!" I shot him shade as I brought my hand up to my cheek. I could feel the flame of pain and knew he'd reddened it. "The sirens need me to be pretty, or they won't take my skin."

The man shook his head. I could see tears in his eyes. "Can you hear yourself? You are talking about cutting your own skin off, mutilating your own body. Can't you see that none of this is real?"

"This is the most real I've ever felt." I don't know why I was even talking to him, why I felt the need to explain. "I'd gladly pull my skin from my body now if they were here."

"Erica, I love you." He leaned forward and kissed me. Something inside me shifted, my mind whirled with emotions that I didn't understand, and my heart pumped blood around my body so quickly that I thought I might faint. He pulled back and looked into my eyes. I could see the expectation in them, but I didn't know what he wanted from me.

"Go away!" I screamed at him. "Leave me be."

I'd never seen anyone look so panicked in all my life, but it was hardly my concern. I just knew I needed him to leave before the sirens came back. I didn't want anything to spoil what was going to happen tonight.

"Please, Erica. It's me. You know me. Tell me my name." He kneeled before me, his top half out of the water and the tip of his tail still wet from the ocean water below me.

"No!" I lied. I did know him, but I couldn't answer him. Something was stopping me. I felt confused, and all my thoughts were thick like mud.

"Tell me my name!" he screamed loudly. His voice echoed around the strange room filling my senses.

"Ari!" I screamed back, tears filling my eyes. "Your name is Ari."

I could sense the others watching me. I knew I appeared weak now that I'd given this stranger what he wanted.

"Leave me be, Ari. Go away."

He slumped as I tried to kick him away from me. If the others told the siren that a stranger was trying to kidnap me, they might not want me anymore, and the thought of that was inconceivable.

"Kiss him," Ari said his voice much softer now. He pointed to the man beside me. I'd already forgotten his name, but I knew he was an enemy. They all were. This was a competition, and I needed to win. I needed to be the one that the siren wanted.

I looked at the strange man in front of me. Tears were running down his face.

"Why should I kiss him? I have no more desire to kiss him than I did you."

I saw him wince at my words for which I was glad. Kicking him hadn't hurt him, but telling him I hadn't wanted to kiss him had been like a knife to the chest. Knowing this, gave me the upper hand. I gave a sly smile and raised my eyebrows waiting for his answer.

He leaned forward and whispered in my ear. "Your kiss will weaken him. He will fall in love with you, and the sirens will not want him anymore."

I liked that. The less of these people there were, the better for me. I needed the sirens to want me more than the others. I couldn't articulate why, but I knew that the sirens had to want me the most.

I turned to the man beside me and grabbed his face between my hands. Leaning forward quickly, I pressed my lips against his. No sooner had our mouths connected than I got a searing pain right through my chest. I held on, fighting the pain, but like swords through my flesh, it quickly consumed me. I fell back on the rocks, clutching my chest and tried to get my breath back.

All at once, everything made sense. The sirens had filled our minds with a spell designed to make us love them, to do anything for them.

"Erica!"

A face appeared above mine. A face I'd been dreaming about for weeks. His wet hair dripped around my face, but it was his falling tears that wet my face.

"It's me," I whispered. "I'm here."

He leaned forward and kissed me, and unlike the kiss with the siren or the kiss with Josh, this was real. Nothing compared to it. Weeks away from him had been the loneliest time of my life, and I knew that nothing was worth being separated from him. Not blind dates with TV adventurers and not even a kingdom.

"What happened?" I could guess most of it. I'd felt his presence almost the whole way here, and the spell that the sirens had put on us was obvious now that I was no longer in the midst of it.

"I hoped kissing you would break you from the spell."

"But I kissed Josh." I turned to look at him. He was staring off into space with a glassy look in his eyes. "I can't say I enjoyed it." I turned back to Ari again, so glad to see him, to be near him.

"When you didn't come to see me for weeks, I thought you'd given up on us. We weren't officially dating so..."

"So you found yourself a girlfriend?"

He looked so ashamed, but I could hardly blame him. He was right that I didn't see him for weeks. My life had been taken over with royal duties and getting out to the sea was impossible.

"Not quite. I very stupidly tried kissing a friend of mine in the hope I could exorcise my feelings for you. I figured that if you didn't want me, I had to find a way to get on with my life."

My heart was breaking in two as he spoke. I did want him. I'd always wanted him.

"What happened?" I didn't tell him that I'd seen him with the girl. What was the point?

"When I kissed her, my insides felt like they were on fire. I'd never felt agony like it. To add insult to injury, the girl slapped me and told me she wasn't interested in me like that."

He laughed quietly and shook his head. "I was such an idiot, but that's how I knew that if you kissed someone else, you'd feel the pain too. We are bonded to each other which means we can never be anyone else's."

I held his face in my hands, and despite the tears that were streaming down my face, I managed a smile. "It's a good thing I like you then."

He laughed again, but this time, I could see he meant it.

"I'm sorry for hurting you, but it was the only way."

"It's fine...It's more than fine." I pulled him closer and kissed him again. From that moment, I knew I'd never be apart from him again.

Enchanted

"We need to get everyone free," I said, glancing around me. Now that the spell had been broken, the upside down ship was not the beautiful, enchanting place I'd taken it for. Now that I could see it through my own eyes, the wood was rotten, seaweed and algae covered the rocks, and the air was stale with the smell of rotten fish. Glancing to the side of me, I could see the others sitting there, blank expressions on their faces and smiles on their lips.

Ari swam off, disappearing under the water, coming back less than a minute later with a sharp rock in his hand.

"This might help get the manacles off."

I stretched the chain between Josh and me tight and laid it flat on a rock. Ari brought his rock down with force time and time again as I pulled. It wasn't helping that Josh was doing everything in his power to stop Ari from unchaining him. Ari was being kicked, hit, and spat on, and still, he continued.

"This is impossible," I moaned after almost an hour of exertion. The rock had smashed, but the chain was steadfastly still together. Ari's arms were covered in bruises from Josh's feet, and he'd been too slow to dodge a blow to the face that had left him with a bloody lip.

"We can't give up, because those things will be back tonight and they will take your body parts. The others might give theirs freely because of the spell, but don't think that because you aren't under their spell anymore, they won't take parts of you. I give up now, and you'll die. All of you will die."

"The ship!" I don't know why I hadn't thought of it before. There were bound to be some tools on the ship somewhere. "Check below decks and the bridge. See if you can find a saw or bolt cutters."

Ari reached forward, kissed me quickly, and dove under the surface of the water. With a flick of his tail, he was gone. I waited ten minutes, watching the others. Shouting to them made no difference, so I sat silently. After an hour had passed, all hope had left me. It shouldn't have taken so long. Even if he couldn't find any tools, he would have come back and let me know. There was no doubt in my mind that he'd been captured. Pain had caused the spell to break on me, but I didn't know how to cause that much pain on the others without damaging them. Josh sat next to me and was the only one in reach anyway. I figured if I could wake him up, maybe he could do the same to the others. I tried nipping his arm, but that only ended up with him slapping me in the face.

"Don't bruise my skin. The sirens need it!" He yelled at me with tremendous anger in his expression, but then, he turned and began to stare out into space again. It was hopeless. Nothing I said to any of them made any difference, and time dragged on. With each minute that passed, any hope that we'd make it out alive left me. It wasn't only our lives at stake. It was my mother lying in the palace infirmary, my grandfather, and the people of Havfrue. Not only had I failed in my mission, I'd failed spectacularly. As I looked at the people next to me, anger began to build. Josh who had come here to prove that sirens existed, Seth that had followed him. He didn't even have his camera with him. He must have left it on the ship. For them, all this had come to nothing. The legend of the sirens would remain a legend, a myth. As for Astrid and Hayden, they'd not signed up for this. I'd dragged them along on this ridiculous adventure when they should have been having the happiest times of their lives. And Ari. He was near. I could feel him, but he'd not returned to the cave. Something had prevented him.

Ari?

I spoke to him in my mind, but there was no answer. Fear ran through me. He was alive, I knew that, but I could think of no reason for him not to answer me.

The pressure in my head due to anger was like a pressure cooker. All the pent-up emotion I'd been feeling for weeks was rising to the top. The royal duties, the media, the sickness, and now this. I opened my mouth and screamed. The noise echoed around inside the upturned boat causing the others to cover their ears from the noise. Weeks of anger and stress tumbled out of my mouth increasing in decibels but making me feel so much better. I emptied my lungs of air and shut my mouth as the echoes died down. It had done no good, not that I thought it would. The others were still glassy-eyed from the spell. We were all going to die and be used for body parts, not that I could understand why. Unlike the sea witch, these women were already perfect in every way.

As I was pondering such things, the surface of the water began to move. The disturbance was caused by two of the sirens who surfaced. I quickly sat straight and stared out ahead of me like the others.

"See, I told you they were all still here," one of them snapped.

"I heard screaming, I'm telling you."

From the corner of my eye, I saw the first one looking closely at Seth.

"Take me first," he whimpered.

"You can have me. I have great skin," yelled Josh who picked up the sharp stone that Ari had dropped earlier and began to hack away at the skin on his arm.

"That won't be necessary...yet." The siren swam over to him and gently took the stone from his hand. "We will do this tonight. A nice sharp knife will make a much tidier job." Neither of the sirens had even glanced my way, but I knew this was my only chance. I leapt up and, using the chains between my arms, pulled the nearest one's head back and wrapped the chain around her neck.

"Let us go!" I shouted across to the other one who glared at me in shock. "Let us go, or I'll strangle your friend."

From the water, instead of trying to stop me, she winked at me. Long lashes of silver covered her diamond-like eyes. She was so beautiful... perfect.

I shook my head, realizing I was getting suckered in again. Her beauty had dumbfounded me. I remembered what I'd heard Ari saying all those hours ago—shut your eyes. I did just that and tried to think of something other than the ethereal perfection of these strange women. I pictured Astrid and how she'd lost her golden hair to the sea witch. I pictured Hayden who loved her no matter what her hair looked like. I pictured these sirens taking our body parts.

"No!" I screamed. "I won't let you." I pulled on the chain while the siren between my arms made a strangled sound.

Then it wasn't just her I could hear. The water bubbled. I hazarded a glance to see the other sirens coming back. They didn't look angry. Quite the opposite, they had warm smiles on their faces and appeared welcoming. The sight of them soothed me, and I slackened the chain. The siren I'd been holding fell to the ground in front of me and then rolled into the water where she grabbed a rock to right herself. The sirens looked at me. All of them. They were just so utterly beyond anything I'd ever seen before

I was taken aback at how beautiful they all were.

"Take me first," I urged. I needed them to take my body...whichever parts they needed...all of it. With every fiber of my being, I needed to be part of them. Somebody handed me a knife.

I was going to be first. They'd chosen me above the others to be the first to give myself to them. I'd never felt such joy.

I held the knife to the flesh of my arm and watched it dig in. As the first drop of blood trickled down, there was a noise from above. I looked up along with everyone else, but there was nothing there, so I continued to push down with the knife.

The noise happened again, a thwack of something on wood. I could see the confusion on the faces of the sirens as they wondered what was happening. I felt my own pulse quicken, wondering if this noise was somehow going to impede my dream of becoming at one with the sirens. There was a final thwack and sunlight poured through the roof. Ari stood there, peering through the hole, an ax in his hand. He continued to hit at the roof, sending splinters of wood down into the water on top of the sirens. I followed the path of one of the larger pieces as it fell hitting one of the sirens on the head. As I saw the siren in the sunlight,

I gasped. She wasn't the beauty I'd thought her to be. None of them were. As the light from the hole Ari was making got bigger, the patch of sunlight fell on more and more of the sirens.

Far from the stunningly beautiful women we'd all seen, these creatures were grotesque. As the light hit them, their true appearances shone through. As the sea witch had been, these things were made of a mismatch of other people. They had the faces of women, but a lot of the body parts they had taken belonged to men and various sea creatures and birds, leaving them unbelievably strange looking. As the light hit them, they shrieked, turning the water into a bubbling mass of flailing sirens.

They weren't the only ones making noise. Beside me, I could hear the screams and shouts of my crewmates from the ship, and the clinking of chains as the spell was well and truly broken.

Why had I thought these creatures would help us? The sea witch had never done anything to help anyone, not without a price, and it was obvious that these snarling women were not about to either. They wanted our skin, parts of our body, but that was not a price I was willing to pay.

The siren that had brought me here shouted loudly, making her friends quieten down. The silence after the echoing noise of scores of people screaming and wailing was deafening.

It was clear that the sirens were disconcerted about having their true colors revealed and their magic stripped away from them, but it didn't make our situation any better. We were still chained to each other and the wall, and even though the sirens would have to come and take our skin themselves rather than let us do it, the results would be the same. We'd be dead, and our bodies would end up as part of this monstrous circus.

A loud splash in the center of the water caused by something falling covered many of the sirens with water and made me jump. Where the splash had occurred, red water began to float to the surface making this horrific place even more macabre. It took me a few seconds to realize what it was, and when I did, my heart fell. It had been Ari that had either jumped or fallen through the hole he'd made into the water. The red was blood. Blood from his legs. I hadn't seen him for so long, and back then, his legs had been a complete mess. I could only imagine how difficult and painful it must have been to climb up the outside of this overturned wrecked ship and do what he did. I watched the spot where he had landed, as did everyone else and waited with bated breath for him to surface.

A Revelation

A whole minute passed before his head breached the surface and as soon as it did, the sirens jumped on him.

"Stop!" I shouted out, my voice echoing around the chamber. "You want something from us, and we need something from you. I know you would prefer to trade rather than have the messy job of pulling our limbs from our bodies yourselves."

It was ok, me speaking these words, but I had literally no idea what to trade with these people. All they seemed to want was us dead so they could use our bodies in various nefarious ways. At least, they had let Ari go in order to listen to what I had to say. He swam over to me and rested on the rocks by my feet.

Are you ok? I asked silently. He nodded in the affirmative, but I could see how tired he was. Doing what he did had really taken it out of him.

"I'm intrigued," the leader said, swimming over to me. How I had ever thought her beautiful was beyond me. They certainly knew some potent magic. In reality, her skin was mottled brown, and her hair was more seaweed than anything else. One of her eyes had almost rotted away entirely leaving a gaping hole through her eye socket. Looking at her was enough to make anyone sick, but I held her gaze. I needed her to know that despite the positions we were in, I wasn't scared of her. It was a trick my father had taught me years ago. He's said that no matter how nervous I was, I should never show it. It was easy to say when you weren't chained up by a psychopathic water creature that wanted nothing more than to strip my skin from my body.

"I wondered why you came here. You want something from us?"

"I do. One of your people put a spell on everyone she ever helped. A few months ago she died, but the spell didn't die with her. My family, my friends...hundreds of people are dying, and we don't have the magic needed to stop it."

The siren laughed. "And you want me to stop this spell? In exchange for what? I think you already know what I want...what we all want." She gestured to the other sirens behind her. They all nodded their heads, showing horrible spiky teeth as they grinned. If I'd had breakfast, at this point, I would have lost it.

"I want us to be able to leave here safely with all our body parts intact. That being said, what else can I give you in exchange for our lives and some of your magic?" Even as I said it, I knew that I sounded ridiculous. I was hardly in a position to barter. "I'm a queen. I have gold. The ship we came on has some riches, but if you let us go, I can make sure more is brought back to you."

She shook her head. "What use have I for gold? We have no shops on this island to spend it. There is nothing you have that I desire that can't be found right here."

She swam closer to me, taking a lock of my hair in her hand. Up close she smelled as disgusting as she looked. I held my breath and tried to come up with a solution to this impossible situation. As it was, I didn't have to. It was Josh that saved the day.

"Fame!" he said. The siren let go of my hair and shifted sideways until she was opposite him.

"I do not think fame will suit me, I do not have the face for television...not yet anyway." She glanced back my way which made me shudder.

"Not fame for you," Josh continued. "I'm famous."

"I don't see how that helps me in any way, shape, or form, and I'm getting tired. I do not care for anything you have to offer."

"No one knows you exist," Josh said hurriedly. "I'm here doing a documentary to prove to the world that you exist. If you'd not caught Seth while he was sleeping, you'd have seen the camera we brought with us. I wouldn't have to show you on screen. I think that you would not like that, but if I showed hints of you...the parts that are...undamaged. An odd tail here, a wing there, I could pique the interest of the people in all the nine kingdoms."

"So what?" she asked. I was wondering the same thing myself.

Josh moved closer to her so they were only inches apart. I don' t know how he could stand it. He was either a much better bluffer than I was, or the sight and smell of her really didn't repulse him the same way it did me.

"It will bring people here. So many people. Look around you. There are so many more of you than there are of us. It doesn't take a genius to see that we won't go very far. Plus, most of the crew is male. As you are all female, surely you would prefer prettier faces than these ugly mugs."

I could see she was thinking about it. Of everyone on the ship, there were only four of us that were women. Astrid, Captain Howell, one of the servants, and myself. There was no way all of them would be able to use us.

"Fine, but I have no reason to trust you. You can all go back to your ship, but I will keep this one here as collateral. I like her hair." She looked back at me, and I had to swallow back vomit. "If she is indeed the queen like she says she is, then I think you will have to stick to your word."

"No!" Ari jumped between her and me, not that he needed to. She wasn't going to attack me, not just then anyway.

Josh remained calm, much calmer than Ari. I grabbed Ari's hand and immediately a flush of excitement and happiness ran through me. Even though my life was in such danger, the magic of the bonding took away the fear. If only we could have harnessed that magic, then we wouldn't be in this situation in the first place.

"That's not going to work," Josh stated plainly. Getting back to our land will take a couple of days. Then, we will have to edit the footage we take of you which could take a week at the very least. On top of that, I'll have to persuade my bosses to air the footage as quickly as possible. I don't think that will be a problem because you'll be sensations, but there is no way Erica would survive long enough. You don't need fresh water to survive, but she does. She'll need food, and her human stomach won't be able to digest the uncooked fish you eat. She'd be dead long before the people started showing up."

"Hmmm."

"But..." Josh added hurriedly sensing he was losing her interest. "Why don't you come back with us? You can stay by my side and watch while I edit the footage to make sure I keep to my word."

I could see her weighing up his proposal. It was ideal for us, but I couldn't see her going for it. She had no guarantee we wouldn't kill her the second we were away from her people.

"Fine," she agreed, shocking me. "I will allow you all to go free to your ship. You will stay at anchor while you and your cameraman come back and film us. Tomorrow we will set sail to your land."

The surprised expression on Josh's face told me that he hadn't expected it to work any more than I had.

I leaned towards him and whispered excitedly. "I could kiss you!"

He winked. "I told you, you'd be begging to kiss me before the end of this trip."

I was too happy to be finally leaving this prison to be annoyed. If anything, I found it funny.

The manacles chaining us together suddenly opened by magic and just like that, we were free. The others were led out through the water by the sirens, but I was allowed to be pulled out by Ari. Being so close to him made me realize just how much I'd missed him. I knew that I had missed him, but swimming here next to him was like coming home.

Part of me wanted him to keep swimming. The two of us could literally swim off into the sunset, and it would be wonderful, but I knew I couldn't leave the others. They'd all done so much for me, ditching them now would be the worst thing I could do, and I'd regret it. Even so, I was reluctant to leave Ari and climb back onto the ship, and there was no way that I was going to let him come aboard. He only needed to be out of the water for a minute before his tail turned into legs and I'd seen the amount of blood he'd lost when he fell into the water earlier. That was undoubtedly from his legs. The sirens, however, didn't care that Ari couldn't go aboard. They only cared that I did. I was forced from him which damn near broke my heart. I'd be able to speak to him over the railings, but it was hardly the same thing. Once I was on deck, I noticed that all the sirens had surrounded us. There was no way they were going to let us sail off in the middle of the night. At least, they stayed in the water. I couldn't bear having them on the ship too.

Seth trooped past me with his camera in his hand. His expression was clear that he wasn't happy to have to go back with the sirens. As the camera wasn't waterproof, he and Josh ended up sitting on a craggy outcrop while the lead siren and a couple of others played about in the water. I watched them for a few minutes wondering how on earth they were going to make the hideous creatures appear beautiful. It was a shame their magic didn't work in the light, but Seth could hardly film in the dark.

Hayden rushed past me with a bucket on a rope, closely followed by Astrid and a couple of servants. They all had buckets too.

"Anyone want to tell me what's going on?" I asked as they threw the buckets over the side. "Are you trying to kill the sirens, because I think you'll need more than empty buckets."

"We're bringing Ari on board. We just need to fill one of the baths with salt water, and he'll be fine."

Of course, he would. How had I not thought about that? He'd done it before in the palace. When the bath was full, Hayden climbed down the rope ladder and hauled Ari over his shoulder. Ari was the bigger of the two, and it was clear that Hayden was struggling, but eventually, he managed to throw him up onto the deck. From there, we had to work quickly to beat the magic that would transform him. Astrid, the servants and I picked him up, sharing the load equally and rushed him to the bath.

The water barely covered his tail, but it was enough. Had the bath been any bigger, I'd have climbed right in there with him. As it was, I had to make do with lying on the wooden floor beside him and holding his hand. It was enough. It was everything.

I could quite happily have lain there on the floor just being in his company, but there was too much to talk about. Things that couldn't wait.

"I came here to ask the sirens about stopping the spell the sea witch cast. My mother is sick, my grandfather too." As I looked at Ari something occurred to me. "Everyone who had help from the sea witch is affected. How come you aren't?"

He looked tired, exhausted even, which was hardly a surprise after the journey he'd just completed, but it was nothing compared to how my mother and grandfather had looked the last time I'd seen them.

"I am affected...Erica...I'm dying."

Ari

I stared at him, not comprehending his words. How could he be dying? He didn't look ill.

"You can't see it when I have my tail," he explained "I look almost normal, but I can feel it. At first, I thought it was just the original curse the witch placed upon me, but the pain I felt when I had legs came even when I had a tail. It's not nearly as bad when I'm like this, but I can feel it. It's like a sickness invading me, and now it's getting higher and higher. When I changed back there, I found I was right. My skin was slewing off much higher up my body than before. It wasn't isolated to my legs."

"I saw the blood," I murmured, tracing a hand up his chest. The skin there appeared normal at first glance, but as I looked a little closer, I could see a very slight discoloring as if there was something sinister going on underneath.

"How far up does it go?" I asked, peering closer, trying to see in the dim light.

He took a deep breath. It reminded me of the time the hospital director told me my father was dead. That deep breath was almost certainly a sign it was going to be bad news "It's almost up to my neck."

The implication was clear. When it reached his head, he'd be completely consumed by it and would die. I could hardly bear it. Not only had we managed to get ourselves into more trouble with the sirens, they still hadn't agreed to use their magic to heal everyone, and I knew they wouldn't. Not without a sacrifice. They wanted people. Josh had promised them lots of people, but that was weeks away, and Ari, my mother, and my grandfather didn't have weeks. They had days at most and looking at Ari, maybe not even that. I could see the magic moving about under his skin. It was faint, but it was there.

I'd tried sacrificing myself for Ari before, and my grandfather had saved me. This time my grandfather wasn't around to stop me. I waited until he fell asleep and crept out of the bathroom. I was going to find the leader and offer myself up in exchange for curing Ari. I couldn't live without him. I knew that now. The pain would be unbearable. This way, he would survive. The leader liked my hair; maybe I could get her to cure my mother too.

I perched on the edge of the deck, looking overboard. Josh and Seth were nowhere to be seen, so presumably, they were back on the ship having shot enough footage. The sun was beginning to lower in the sky, and the sirens kept guard in the water below.

I was just about to fling myself over when I was grappled to the floor. It was Ari, and the two of us skidded for a way and then fell overboard anyway.

As we hit the water, all I could see was blood, and it was obvious who it belonged to. Wrapping my arms around his waist, I pulled him to the surface. His chest was raw and bloody, and below the ocean surface, I could feel he still had legs. Something had happened to stop the magic that brought his tail back.

He didn't make a sound when I pulled him up to a rock. He drifted in and out of consciousness, his eyes flickering.

"Why did you change? Why did you come after me?"

"You forget I can see your thoughts when you are near," he gave me a small smile and then his eyes closed. He'd known I was trying to save him, and he'd decided to save me instead. I screamed loudly, shouting out his name, but his eyes remained closed. All my screaming did was bring most of the people on the ship to the deck and alert the sirens. Within a minute of me getting onto the rock, we were surrounded by them. Looking up, I could see my friends on the ship.

"Help me!" I shouted to no one in particular. "Ari is dying."

"We do not care," the leader said, swimming through the other sirens. "His body is of no use to us. Look at him. Leave him here on the rocks and let the birds have him."

How easily she dismissed him.

"No!" I will not go back without him. You need to heal him, or all this is over."

She glared at me. "I'm already doing you a favor by not taking your bodies now. I do not see why I should do you any more favors. I should kill you now."

"Kill her, and this ship goes up in flames."

We all looked up to see Hayden with a gas lamp in his hand. He was poised, ready to smash it onto the wooden deck. When Astrid saw what he was doing, she ran back and got another one.

"Everyone on this ship will burn. You'll get nothing except Erica."

"No!" she screeched, seeing her prize almost slip away. "I will save him, but only him. I know there are others in your land and I will not extend my magic to them."

"Do it!" I demanded. I'd figure out a way to help the others back home later, now Ari's plight was dire. His breathing was shallow, and his body was a bleeding pulpy mass. He didn't have much time.

The leader spread her wings. Even they looked like a poorly put together mess of mismatched feathers taken from numerous seabirds. She took off into the sky and flew over the island.

"Where is she going?" I asked in a panic, cradling Ari's head in my arms.

"Do not fear," snapped one of the nearby sirens, showing green furry teeth, "She is going to get the magic."

Get the magic? I'd assumed it was within her, that these sirens were magical beings. I'd certainly been a victim of their magic. Not that I cared. I was just happy that something was to be done to help Ari. I stroked his face, and as I did, I watched the disease work its way up his neck.

I tapped my toe upon a rock impatiently, desperate for the lead siren to come back with whatever it was she needed to save him. If she didn't get back soon, it would be too late. Ari's face was wet with my tears, but salt water alone could not heal his wounds.

"Come on, come on," I whispered under my breath as if it would hurry the siren up. The disease was up to his chin now, and there was nothing I could do to stop it. My stomach churned as I watched the insidious line of red get higher and higher. No medicine in any of the kingdoms could help him now. Magic was his only chance of survival, and then, only if it came in time. I searched the dimming skies for her and grazed my eyes over the island I'd barely looked at since getting here. I had no reason to as the sirens lived on the rocks and in the water surrounding it, but now as I looked, I could see it was a bleak place with patches of grass, sand, and rocks, and not much else. I could only see part of the island, but it was not a large place. We could have sailed around the whole thing in a couple of hours if we had chosen to. Beyond it, there were more islands that looked the same. Barren, desolate places that suited the weird sirens very well.

A light appeared in the sky. My heart lifted when I saw it was the lead siren. She was glowing; her body appeared like an early star in the evening sky, getting bigger as she approached. She'd gone back to her beautiful self. Like an angel descending from heaven, she touched down beside us. Despite her current form, she was not using her magic to pull us in. I did not have the desire to cut my body for her, to be part of her as I had the night before. I looked for something in her hands, the thing that was causing her magic, but her hands were empty. She placed them on Ari's chest and immediately the skin there healed. With each inch of Ari's skin that came back to life, her light dimmed a little. By the time she got to his legs, her light was almost out, but she persisted. His legs grew scales and then became one until he was whole again. The perfect specimen of a merman. He opened his eyes as the lead siren fell to the rocks beside him.

"What happened?" asked Ari sitting up. He no longer looked tired, and his color had returned to normal. I wanted to fling myself upon him, but the siren needed help. It would have been so easy to leave her, but she'd brought Ari back to me, and now she was suffering. I pulled her into my arms, the same way I'd done with Ari just moments before.

215

Unlike Ari, she was breathing normally, but her eyes were closed. Her beauty had completely faded, and she was back to being her normal self. I didn't let that stop me. I was so grateful to her for saving Ari that I hugged her closely. She received the same amount of my tears that Ari had as I tried to wake her. The other sirens stayed in the water, but they watched me closely.

"Please come back!" I whispered to her, stroking her misshapen face. She'd done a lot of wrong, but in the end, if it wasn't for her, Ari would already be dead.

Ari pulled himself around to her other side and held her as I took off my jacket and laid it on her. It was still damp, but at least it kept the wind off her. I couldn't understand why the other sirens were doing nothing to help her. Neither Ari nor I had any magic to do anything but after a few minutes, her one good eye fluttered open. She looked at me with such a curious expression before sitting up. My jacket fell down around her waist. She picked it up, held it in her hands, feeling the fabric then handed it back to me.

"Go back to your ship," she commanded. She stood up without looking back at me and Ari and dived straight into the water. The other sirens followed her, disappearing into the depths.

The whole thing piqued my curiosity, but I was so thrilled to have Ari back to normal that I didn't think on it for too long. He was completely healthy again, and judging by the expression on his face, in good spirits.

"I'd forgotten what it was like to not be in pain. Even when I had my tail, the magic weighed me down. Until it was lifted, I hadn't realized just how much."

"You still have your tail now," I pointed out.

He looked down and grinned. "I know."

He hadn't grasped what I was getting at. "Your tail is dry. You are out of water. You no longer have legs."

He looked down again. "The siren took all the magic, not just the magic that affected me in a bad way. I'm back to how I was before I had any dealings with the sea witch."

I scooted over to him, and he wrapped me in his arms. It was just like coming home.

"Get a room!" Someone shouted from the ship deck. I recognized Josh's voice.

"Exactly who is that?" Ari asked, glancing up at the deck.

I grinned. "I'll introduce you properly, come on."

Hayden had to climb back down the rope ladder to bring Ari back up again. It was in fine spirits that we all headed inside to eat our first meal in hours.

The servants had done a marvelous job of making dinner, and for the first time since starting the trip, everyone, including all the crew, sat around the huge dining table and ate together.

The atmosphere was almost party-like as we toasted to Ari's health. His return to fine health affected me too in ways I had never expected. I felt lighter than I had in weeks. I'd not felt any pain, not in the same way as Ari had, but my body had felt heavier, slower. Now that he was better I felt as though I would float off my seat if I didn't hold onto it. It was just another of the weird and wondrous ways the magic of the bonding held us together. I breathed easier knowing it was all over.

"The sirens aren't surrounding the ship anymore," pointed out Captain Howell. She was the only one who had refused a glass of wine citing the fact she was in charge of the ship, and she couldn't do that without all her faculties about her.

"If they've gone, why don't we leave now before they come back?" Hayden asked the people around the table.

Almost everyone was in agreement, but something didn't rest easy with me. For a start, going home without a way to help my mother was not an option. Now I'd seen how quickly Ari was saved, I needed to figure a way to get help for the others too. Plus there was the fact that the lead siren hurt herself in saving Ari. It might have been temporary, but she'd given everything she had. It would have been much easier to let him die. Many of the sirens had wings, and so if Astrid and Hayden had set the ship on fire, the sirens would have been able to fly up and grab them all before they burned to death. Plus, I think it was quite obvious that Hayden was bluffing. He wasn't particularly good at it. No, something else had made her save Ari. Despite everything, I saw compassion there. If there was even an ounce of compassion in her, there was a chance she would help the others.

I put this theory to everyone around the table. Most shook their heads.

"She wasn't showing much compassion when she had us chained up and was ready to cut our skin off," Hayden reminded me.

"No, she didn't. But think about it. These women don't get married and have children. They are all female. They are ancient beings that stay alive for centuries by taking body parts from others. Without being able to do that, the whole species would die out. If you were in the same situation, what would you do?"

Hayden shrugged, but I could tell he was thinking about it.

"I never thought about it that way," Astrid replied glumly. "It must be awful watching your body fall apart due to old age and yet you keep on living."

"I don't think they are inherently bad people. They are doing what they must do to survive," I added.

"Well, I, for one, don't want to help their species survive by giving them any of my limbs," Hayden argued, standing up and throwing his napkin down on his empty plate. "I think we should go while we can."

"Actually I disagree," Josh asserted, joining in the conversation.

Hayden rolled his eyes. "Of course you do," he replied, his voice dripping in sarcasm. He held his hand out to Astrid who took it. She gave me an 'I'm sorry' look as she followed him to the door.

"You are obviously going to do whatever you want despite the fact that this is supposed to be Astrid's and my honeymoon. Funnily enough, when you offered me this ship, I wasn't expecting you to come with us and bring us to somewhere so dangerous."

I opened my mouth to answer him, but he was already gone, taking Astrid with him.

"Don't listen to him," Josh said. "He doesn't know what he's saying. You did what you had to do."

I sighed. Josh was wrong. Hayden had every right to be unhappy with me. Not that I could do anything about it at the moment.

"Why do you think we should stay?" I asked Josh. I knew my reasons, but I was interested to learn what the great adventurer had to say on the matter.

"I think we should stay the night because I think I've found a way to save your friends and family.

The First Time

I tried to get more information out of Josh, but he refused to say any more on the subject. After dinner, though, I noticed that he made sure both Seth and his camera were with him when he left the dining room. Apart from the problem with Hayden and upsetting his honeymoon, I felt amazingly wonderful. Ari was back with me, and Josh had made claims that he could save everyone else. I had to ask a couple of members of staff to carry Ari to my bedroom, but once we were there, I shut the door behind us and left the world outside.

He lay on the bottom bunk as getting him up to the top bunk where I'd been sleeping would have been too difficult a task.

Now that we were together and alone, a fit of nerves overcame me. I'd been dreaming of this moment for so long, but now it was here, I wasn't sure how to act, or what to do.

"Are you ok?" Ari asked as I dithered by the sink, cleaning my teeth and making a huge show of wiping my mouth on a towel. I'd forgotten just how good-looking he was. My insides squirmed just looking at him. He was completely naked which wasn't helping my insides one bit. I'd seen him naked before. He lived in the sea, he was almost always sans clothes so to speak, but now that we were alone in my room, his nakedness was so much more apparent, so much more out there. I'd slept next to him when he had legs, but this was something different entirely. My whole body shook with nerves as I began to undress. His eyes never left mine as I pulled my t-shirt over my head. My skin felt rough with the salt from the sea water I'd allowed to dry there. I kept my eyes locked onto his and took a deep breath as I pulled my trousers down, quickly followed by my underwear.

Just as he had appeared more naked than usual, I had never felt so undressed in my life. I stood completely still as he raked his eyes down my body.

"Come to me."

My heart thumped wildly as I laid myself on the bed next to him. I had missed him so much, and I wanted him so badly.

I shifted my position so his arm was under my head and his chest was touching mine. With him so close to me, everything was right with the world. Our bonding had never been so apparent to me as it was now. I could feel the rhythm of his heart and even though he appeared a lot calmer than I felt, his beat matched mine, a percussion of souls. Whatever magic this was, it hadn't been stripped away by the siren's spell.

I ran my hand down his chest, marveling at the curvature of his muscles, hardened by years of swimming through the ocean.

His tail wrapped around my legs, shuffling my lower half closer and increasing the rate of my breathing. I was completely entwined in his body, and though we were out of the ocean now, I felt as though I was drowning in him.

I'd run through the whole gamut of emotions with him since whatever magic it was brought us together and bonded us, but never in my life had I been taken to such highs as he was taking me now. He kissed me slowly along my neckline, looking up occasionally to see if I was ok with it. As he began to kiss lower, I closed my eyes, letting out a soft moan as his lips touched the skin on my abdomen, leaving a trail of salty kiss marks over my skin. My first time was not the experience I'd been expecting.

Mainly, because I'd not known such emotions, such feeling existed at all.

I didn't know what to expect. He was a merman and I...well I was human. Anatomically we didn't match up. Our minds and our souls fitted together perfectly as though we were made for each other, but unless we found a way for him to become human or for me to be a full mermaid, our bodies were never going to mesh in the right way. And yet we found a way to make it work for us and afterwards, he held me tightly as I couldn't stop shaking. I could barely control the magnitude of my emotions, and it was only when he softly stroked my hair and whispered words of love to me that I got my heart rate down enough to sleep.

Overboard

The ship was a hive of activity the next morning. I didn't have to leave the little piece of heaven I'd found, snuggled in the crook of Ari's arm to hear it.

Someone whistled a merry tune as they passed by my door, and I could hear the crew setting the dining hall up for breakfast.

"We should probably get up," commented Ari lazily. "It sounds like we are the last two in bed."

I snuggled in deeper, relishing the warmth of his body next to mine. "I like it that way," I replied. "I might stay here all day and let everyone else get on with it."

Ari pulled his arm up, taking my head with it and kissed me on the forehead. After last night, I was sure I'd used up my quota of flutters, but sure enough, butterflies began to swarm in my stomach, and my heart began to beat that little bit quicker.

Unfortunately, there was a knock on the door. It seemed that Ari wasn't the only one who thought I should get my ass out of bed.

"Acania wants to speak to you." It was Josh.

I scrunched up my nose trying to remember who Acania was. I mentally listed the crew's names in my head, but as far as I was aware, there wasn't an Acania among them.

"Just a minute!"

Pulling myself away from Ari, I found a clean dress and slipped it over my head. Ari pulled a sheet over himself as I opened the door.

"Woah, sorry for interrupting." Josh winked and grinned in a very Josh-like manner, not seeming sorry at all. "The best man won, huh?"

"Josh, I hate to break this to you, but there was never a competition. If there had been a competition for my affections, you would not have been in the running."

Josh clicked his tongue but kept the grin on his face. "I remember that time in the upturned boat that you begged me to kiss you."

I rolled my eyes. "I think begging is a strong word. Who is Acania?"

"Oh!" Josh stood up straight, now that he wasn't making suggestive comments. "She's that siren you saved."

My eyebrows shot up. What reason could she possibly have to speak to me?

"She's waiting upstairs." Josh extended his index finger and pointed up. He lowered his voice. "She was quite calm and almost normal when she asked to come aboard, except for that rotten smell and that weird eye of hers." He gave an involuntary shiver.

"Can you help Ari get upstairs for breakfast? I'll go and speak to her."

I left him to figure out the logistics of carrying a merman to the upper deck and headed up to meet Acania. We were due to leave for home this morning with a fleet of sirens behind us. I wondered what had changed. I hoped that whatever it was, it had something to do with helping the people of Havfrue. It was the one thing that plagued me about this trip. I'd managed to figure out how to free us from the sirens, but I hadn't accomplished what I'd set out to do. On top of that, the sirens would be coming with us causing more problems and Hayden was still angry with me for ruining his honeymoon. The only good thing to come from this was the fact I had Ari back, and he was finally cured of his illness. All this was going through my mind as I entered the dining room. The others were already there eating breakfast, but Acania was nowhere to be seen. Astrid pointed to the door that led out onto the deck.

Outside, the weather had turned. The wind from last night had picked up considerably, and sea spray wet the decks. I wished I'd put on something more substantial than a summer dress, but Acania didn't seem to notice the weather. She must have heard me coming, but she continued to look out to sea.

"Good morning," I uttered, standing next to her by the railing. I could taste the salt in the wind, and within seconds my hair was soaked through. Acania nodded her head but remained silent. I wondered if I was supposed to start the conversation, but without knowing what she was here for, I wasn't sure what to say.

"Are your people ready to go? I wanted to set off early." I started. I was hoping to have a conversation about her magic and bringing it with us, but it couldn't be the first thing I said to her.

She looked out over the foaming ocean "My people are not going."

"Oh?" I was surprised. That had been her reason for letting us go.

"You tried to save me last night. After everything I had done to you and your friends."

"You saved Ari's life!" I pointed out. "If it hadn't been for you, he would have died."

"Yes. You should know that I only did it because he is a creature of the sea like me. Had he been human I would have let him rot."

I took in this information. "The sea witch who caused his disease in the first place didn't care that he was a merman. Everyone who is affected by her spell is a merperson."

"I knew her. This sea witch you talk about. She lived here with us a long time ago. Her name was Ursula, and she hated what we had all become. We were once young and beautiful. We lured the ships onto the rocks with nothing but our beauty and our singing. Back then, we only desired company. The sailors we lured to our islands would come and party with us. We had the most amazing times, and when they had to leave, we let them go willingly. Many came back after they had completed their missions, they liked us so much. We had no need for magic."

She became silent once again.

"What happened?" I couldn't quite square up the image of those hideous sirens with the thought that anyone would come back willingly.

"Time. Time happened. It was so slow at first that we barely noticed it, but when the sailors stopped coming, we realized how much we had aged. That's when we decided to use our magic, and it was about that time that Ursula left us. She was the one who told us to use the body parts of sailors to stay alive. I was totally against it, so she left. It was a hundred years before I realized she was right. Our bodies had decayed to the point that if we didn't, we wouldn't survive."

"How did you originate? I mean, it's strange for a species to only have females and have no way to procreate."

Acania laughed. He voice was so shrill I almost had to cover my ears.

"You humans think the strangest of things. Do you think we were delivered here right from the gods? I do not believe in such things."

I squirmed, feeling embarrassed at my lack of knowledge. Anthony had been telling me for months that I needed to find out more about the other kingdoms and the beings that lived there. I knew magic existed, why not gods?

"A few months ago I didn't know mermaids existed. It was only recently I found out I was a half-mermaid myself. Two days ago I'd never heard of sirens, and yet, here you are. I've learned to be open-minded."

For the first time since I'd walked on deck, she turned to look at me. I tried not to flinch at her face.

"You are half-mermaid?" She seemed surprised.

"Yes, but I don't have a tail, and I can't breathe underwater on my own. I guess I inherited more of my father's genes than my mother's. It has only been recently that I learned to swim."

"Very little surprises me, but you do. A mermaid that lives on land. That must be difficult."

I thought about my problem with Ari. The fact that he couldn't live on land with me was the biggest difficulty. "As I said, I didn't know any different. I've always lived on land."

She nodded thoughtfully. "There are male sirens. The way we live is not normal for our kind. Usually, the males would live on one island and the females on a neighboring island and once a year we'd meet in the middle to mate. Many hundreds of years ago a storm hit. It was extremely severe. This island has a network of underwater caves in which we were able to shelter. The men of the other island didn't have such a place, and they all perished.

As I told you before, we had the company of passing sailors, but unlike the merfolk, we cannot mate with humans. We can only take their body parts and use them to survive. It is not much of an existence, but it is all we have."

My heart went out to her. Her life sounded miserable. "You said that you aren't coming with us. Why?"

"I will be coming with you. It is my sisters who will stay behind. I know what humans are like. My sisters will be ridiculed and hounded. I will watch over your friends editing and make sure he shows the footage."

My heart sank. The way she had spoken, I had thought she was going to let us go free.

"You still plan to lure people to their deaths?"

"What else can I do?" she asked simply.

I sighed. She was obviously not going to change her mind. It was yet another problem I would have to deal with. At least, I didn't have to worry about the rest of the sirens. I probably should have felt more relief at it only being her, but in the back of my mind, I wondered what her real motive was and if we weren't heading for more trouble.

"Come inside," I invited her. "They are serving breakfast."

I wasn't sure how she would walk, as like Ari, she only had a tail, but she extended her wings and fluttered behind me.

As I opened the door that would take us inside, Captain Howell raised the anchor. I felt the lurch of the ship as it began the long journey back home.

The ship listed from side to side as another serving was brought out to accommodate Acania. I could see the thinly veiled revulsion in the eyes of the server as she piled food onto her plate. I'm sure Acania saw it too. Even with one eye, it was pretty hard to miss. I didn't like the way Acania saw the world, but I could understand it. To be looked at in that way and worse still, to know how awful you looked when you were once one of the most beautiful creatures in the sea, must be a terrible torment.

The rest of the people around the table only looked at her with mild curiosity. I could see that they were dying to know what she had said to me.

"What is this?" she asked, looking down at her plate which had bacon, eggs, sausages and cooked tomatoes on it. She glanced around the table to see if anyone else was eating it. She probably thought we were trying to poison her.

"It's good. Try it," I said, taking my fork and spearing a slice of bacon. She watched me eat it and waited until I swallowed before she was satisfied it wasn't a ruse to kill her. Once she'd taken her first bite, she tucked right in. I guess it made a nice change from raw fish or whatever it was she usually ate.

"What's happening?" Hayden, who was seated next to me, whispered.

I wished I could tell him some better news, but nothing really had changed. "She's still wanting to have Josh air the footage he filmed to lure people there."

I sighed. As a queen, I should have been doing everything in my power to protect my kingdom, and here I was, not even the official monarch yet and actively bringing the enemy to our shores. Maybe Anthony was right. I wasn't really cut out for ruling. I'd certainly not done a great job of it so far.

After breakfast, Acania went outside, braving the howling wind and freezing rain. Through a porthole, I saw her holding onto the railing, gazing out over the stormy ocean in much the same way she had when I'd been out there with her. Not that there was much to see. The cloud was thick and heavy with rain, and everything out there was a shade of gray.

"Let me get this straight," Hayden started as the servants cleared our plates away. "Everyone is still sick, and she won't do anything to help, and yet, she 's coming back with us with the aim of making a TV show about her and her weird friends that will lure many of the people of Trifork back to them so the sirens can murder them for body parts?"

I nodded bleakly. There was no point denying it. In coming out to sea, I'd made the situation worse.

"I bet Josh is loving this," Hayden added grumpily.

I looked around the table. I'd not noticed before, but Josh was missing. "Where is Josh?"

Hayden huffed. "The idiot asked for his food to be taken to his room, but I suppose we are the idiots now. He didn't have to try to force food down while looking at that monstrosity."

"Hayden!" Astrid put her hand on his arm, and he visibly relaxed.

He looked up. "I'm sorry. I'm just feeling frustrated. I wanted this trip to be special, and it's been nothing but a nightmare from start to finish."

"I messed up. It's my fault, but I promise that once this is over, you can take the ship anywhere you want." Even as I said it, I could hear Anthony chastising me. Knowing my luck, in the short time we'd been away, Trifork would have broken out into war or something, and we'd need the ship elsewhere.

"Why don't I go out and talk to her?" Ari offered. "She might listen to me as we both come for the sea. She made the decision to save me after all."

"Why don't you just push her overboard while you're at it?" grumbled Hayden.

Ari smiled "Because she has wings and would fly right back."

The ship rolled as a particularly large wave hit us. Seth stood up, looking rather green and rushed out of the room, more than likely to find somewhere to throw up.

"The storm is really picking up," observed Astrid. "Maybe you should wait until it subsides? She might have wings, but you don't. I'd hate for you to accidentally fall over the side."

"If he fell, he'd be fine. You forget he's a merman. The sea might look turbulent from up here, but below the surface, it will be calm."

As I said it, I noticed some movement through the porthole. It wasn't Ari as he was still sitting beside me, but someone had joined Acania on deck.

I pointed to the window so the others would see what I was seeing.

"What does that imbecile think he's doing?" Hayden shifted slightly to get a better view of what Josh was doing.

He appeared to be trying to reason with Acania. The coat he wore was huge, and it appeared that he was hiding something under it.

Another wave hit us, coming right over the deck. I had to grip the table to keep from falling over. When I looked back outside, both Josh and Acania were gone. They'd both been swept over the side.

"Josh!" Astrid shouted, but it was too late. He was already gone.

Dead Alive

"Guys! Help me up!" Ari demanded.

When I realized what he planned to do, I pulled his arm over my shoulder, wrapped my own arms around his waist and tried to lift him. Astrid ran around the table, quickly followed by Hayden. Between us, we managed to get him outside. The rain lashed down, stinging my skin. I could barely keep my eyes open to look around, but it was clear that there was no one left on the deck.

"Throw me over!" Quickly!"

We heaved Ari up to the railing, but it was him that propelled himself over the edge. I watched as he disappeared under the churning water. Beside me, Astrid gripped the railing tightly as we waited to see Ari resurface.

"Get in here now!"

I could barely hear her over the rain and wind, but her voice just barely lifted over the squall.

"You'll go overboard too if you stay out here."

The huge waves battered the ship, and I had to admit she was right. There was no point in us risking our lives just to see if Ari would save Josh.

We all trooped back into the dining room and shut the door behind us.

Captain Howell looked stern as she addressed the three of us. "I've got the first officer steering this thing, but I don't feel comfortable leaving him alone up there in weather like this. I saw the others go over, but there is nothing you or I can do about it. I can't keep the ship still in this. My only option is to try to get through it as quickly as possible, but I can only do that if you three stay inside and I don't have to worry about you."

Like naughty school children, we nodded our heads.

There was nothing for us to do but wait it out. I knew Ari would be safe. He'd spent his life underwater, but whether he'd find Josh in these choppy waters in time was another matter.

The ship lurched again as another wave hit us. I grabbed the table and held tightly until the ship righted itself, and I could sit in a chair. Opposite me, I could see the fear in Astrid's face and Hayden's. Although he was hiding it much better than Astrid, I'd known him long enough to know he was scared too.

For hours, we sat there as the ship creaked under the pressure of the battering ocean. No food was served as it was impossible to cook in conditions like these, but the servants brought us snacks and drinks to keep us going. The storm lasted almost all day, but eventually, it petered out, and the blue of the sky began to show through the clouds. At that point, Captain Howell let us go outside. Hayden and Astrid retired to their bedroom, but I stepped outside onto the water soaked deck. The sea was back to a beautiful blue from the terrible grey it had been, and we no longer lurched from side to side.

I scoured the horizon and the sea between there and the ship, but there was no sign of Ari or Josh. Acania was also nowhere to be seen.

My emotions spiraled as I didn't know what to think. There was no way of telling whether Josh had survived. I knew Ari was alive. Thanks to our bonding, I could feel him. He felt distant, but I knew in my heart he was alive which gave me some comfort. In the distance, I saw land, and as we got closer, I recognized it as the shoreline of Trifork. We were finally home. It was with mixed feelings that I walked off the boat when we had sailed safely into dock. Acania was no longer with us, which meant I didn't have to deal with the crazy scheme, but I was no closer to finding a cure for my mother or the others. I'd also been away a day longer than expected so there was no telling what I'd find at home.

I left the boat with Hayden and Astrid, telling them that they could do with it as they wished, but they both elected to come back to the palace with me. Instead of waiting for a palace driver to come pick us up, we took a taxi home. Terror filled me as we were driven down the long palace driveway, not knowing what I might find when I got to the end of it. I didn't think I'd cope if my mother had died while I was away.

John must have seen us coming as he was waiting by the front doors as we stepped out of the car.

"Your Highness," he bowed as I ran over to him. He had a grim expression on his face.

"My mother? Is she...?" I couldn't even finish the sentence.

"She is alive, but only just. When you left, Anthony sent some guards to Thalia. Luckily, they met a mage en-route and brought him back here. He's managed to slow the process of whatever it is ailing her, but he cannot stop it nor reverse it."

I nodded. The news was bad, but I was honestly expecting worse. At least she was alive. I thanked John.

"I'm afraid there is some other bad news."

"More bad news?" I felt as though I'd lived a lifetime of bad news in the past few months. What else could possibly have happened?

"Ari arrived back about half an hour ago. I, myself went down to the rocks to speak to him after being alerted to his presence by a guard."

"And?" I knew Ari was alright. I could feel it in my heart.

John cleared his throat. "He asked me to tell you that he couldn't find Josh. He says he tried, but in the rough water, Josh was nowhere to be seen. He says he tried for over an hour but had to give up. He swam back here. He said he'd wait down by the rocks for you for as long as you need. He wants you to spend time with your mother first."

I nodded my head as my throat constricted. Josh had drowned. I barely knew the guy, and there were times he annoyed me, but the pain I felt at hearing he'd died still stabbed me sharply in the chest. He'd done so much for me and for the people of both Trifork and Havfrue.

It was with a heavy heart I headed to the infirmary. I found my mother looking deathly pale, her eyelids purple and her breathing shallow. Next to her sat Anthony and a man I didn't recognize. His hair was long, but thinning on top and he wore horn-rimmed glasses.

Anthony stood up as soon as he saw me. "Did you manage to find the sirens?" I could see the hope in his face that I'd brought a miracle cure home with me.

I opened my mouth but didn't know how to tell him that I'd messed up in an epic fashion. I didn't need to; he read my expression perfectly. His face fell, and he sat back down.

"She's not going to make it, Erica," he said slowly. "This is Clement. He's done everything he can to keep her alive, but he's using all his power. Eventually, he will tire, and then she'll die."

I'm sorry Your Highness, he said standing up and bowing his head. "I wish there was more I could do. This magic is powerful and far beyond my capabilities. I'm using all my energy to keep her alive, but I'm an old man. I cannot compete with whatever magic this is."

"I'm grateful for everything you have done and continue to do. Thank you. Do you have any idea how long you can keep the magic back? If you can hold on for a couple of days, maybe the guards will have found some other magi and brought them back by then."

Both Clement and Anthony shook their heads, and my heart felt like a brick in my chest.

"Your mother has only hours left to live. A day at the very most."

I fell by her side and took hold of her hand. She was so very cold, almost as though she had ice traveling through her veins instead of blood.

I'd failed her in the worst way possible, and I could barely breathe with the pain of losing another parent so soon after losing my father. Yet what could I do? I'd blown my only chance of saving her. Acania was lost at sea somewhere, and she'd already said that she wouldn't help. I laid my head down by her side and rubbed her hand to get some warmth into it. The only sound I could hear was the clock on the wall, counting down the last minutes of my mother's life and the sound of my own heart beating. I stayed like that, cursing the tick after painful tick of the clock until my arm went numb. I didn't cry. I wanted to, but the tears wouldn't come. I only lay there wishing I could speak to her one more time, wishing that she could hear me.

"I think it's time," Clement said solemnly. "My power is dwindling, and I can't keep her here much longer. I'm so sorry, but now you should say your last goodbyes to her."

I lifted my head and looked over at him. He did look tired. He was paler than when I'd first walked in the infirmary. Anthony stood up and kissed our mother on her forehead. I hoped, feeling her son so close to her would make her open her eyes, but they remained steadfastly shut.

"I'm so sorry," I whispered to her. "I tried." I neatened her hair and crossed her hands on her chest before I too bent over to kiss her. I could still feel the light breath of her on my cheek as I kissed her forehead as Anthony had done. She was still alive, but without Clement using his magic, she had minutes left rather than hours. My heart was already shredded with the loss of my father; I wasn't sure how I would cope with losing my mother as well. Since I found out she was a mermaid, I'd been so busy, that I'd not had time to sit and talk to her about her time under the water before she came to land and married my father. Why couldn't I have made time?

The tears finally came. I pulled back quickly, not wanting to dampen her pretty face. She'd always taken so much pride in her looks that I wanted to keep her looking as pretty as she would want. It was the least I could do for her after failing to save her life.

The silence was broken by the sound of shouting coming from the door of the infirmary. Lucy the nurse, who had kept out of our way to let us have our final farewell with our mother stormed past us with a grim expression to shout at whoever was causing the commotion. I watched as she opened the door. Behind it were two men fighting. Actually fighting—punching each other and wrestling. Lucy bellowed at them which scared them both enough to stop what they were doing and look at her. One of them I recognized as a palace guard in uniform. The other was Josh.

Saved

"This man was attempting to get in here," the guard said apologetically. "I'm so sorry to disturb you, Your Highness."

"It's fine. Let him in." My heart jumped at the sight of him. He'd not drowned, but how had he managed to get all the way back here when I'd clearly seen him fall from the ship? Ari hadn't brought him back. He'd not even seen him under the water. I thought back to the size of the waves as he'd been thrown overboard. I couldn't imagine how he'd managed to survive.

Lucy gave him a frown. "Are you sure, Erica? Under the circumstances..."

Josh was still soaking wet and was dripping sea water all over the floor. He looked at me urgently and pointed to his coat. The same coat he'd fallen overboard in.

"It's ok, Lucy."

She moved back to let Josh in, but I could see she wasn't pleased about it.

"My mother is dying," I explained to Josh as he entered the infirmary. I wanted to ask him how he'd survived, how he'd got here so quickly, but my mother's time was running out quickly.

"I know. Why do you think I came here? Why do you think I dodged three palace guards and had to break a window to get to you? Because I knew it would take too long to explain to the guards if I tried getting in through the front door."

"Is this a friend of yours Erica?" piped up Anthony, "Because I think his presence here is highly inappropriate."

For once, I agreed with my brother. I was confused about his being here and ridiculously happy to see that he hadn't drowned, but the truth of the matter was, I had barely any time left with my mother, and I didn't want to waste the little I did have.

"Josh. I'm really happy you are alive. I think Astrid and Hayden are in the palace somewhere. Why don't you find them? I'll ask one of the servants to get you all something to eat and maybe find you a towel and a change of clothes."

Instead of turning back to the door, he opened his coat and pulled out a large iron ring which he threw at my mother's bed, landing just by her hand. With the diameter of a dinner plate, it looked like a wedding ring for a giant except with more rust.

"What do you think you are doing?" Anthony growled, stepping round Clement so he could get to Josh. Before he was even halfway around, the ring began to glow. At first, it was localized to only the ring, but then the warm glow moved into my mother's hand. As it crept up her arm, I turned my head back to Josh. His eyes were closed, and his arms outstretched pointing toward the ring.

"What's happening?" asked Anthony, having lost some of that bluster.

I shook my head, turning my attention back to my mother. "I don't know," I replied, but that wasn't quite the truth. I'd seen this glow before, and I'd felt the warmth it produced and the slight crackle in the air. This was magic. The same magic Acania had used on Ari only now it seemed that it was Josh performing it.

Just as Ari's had, my mother's pale skin got its color back and she no longer looked on the verge of death. As I reached out for her, she took a deep breath and opened her eyes. At the same moment, the light flickered, before going out completely and behind me, Josh fell to the floor.

"Lucy!" I called out, caught between wanting to hug my mother and help Josh. Anthony and Clement ran around my mother's bed and helped me lift Josh onto the bed next to hers as Lucy rushed over. Josh was completely unconscious, but if he was anything like Acania, he would come around soon enough.

"What's happening?" My mother's voice came from the bed behind me. I turned and ran to her side, hugging her so hard, she might burst. The feeling of heat on my arm alerted me to the iron ring. It was glowing red with smoke coming from it.

My mother shifted away from it to keep from burning herself as it singed a black ring on the sheet beneath it.

It was Clement that dealt with it. He shouted out some mumbo jumbo that could have been a magic word, and the ring went back to how it was before my mother had woken up. The faint smell of burning filled the air, and I found myself surrounded by a number of confused people.

"The ring is magic," I said, pointing out the obvious. How it had come to be in Josh's possession and how he'd gotten it here were much more of a mystery.

Clement picked it up with his gloved hand and examined it closely. "This is an extremely powerful magical artifact," he pronounced. "I've never seen anything quite like it before."

As I peered closer to the ring that now looked utterly unspecial, I heard a moaning from behind me. It was Josh waking from his magical slumber.

"Lucy," I called. "Can you give my mother a thorough checkup please?" I needed her away from Josh so I could find out how he'd saved her.

"I'm perfectly fine," my mother fussed, but Lucy ran to get her stethoscope anyway. They were both headstrong women, but I had a feeling that Lucy would manage to win this one.

"Josh." I sat beside him on the bed. His eyes appeared foggy, but after a few moments, they came back into focus.

When he saw me, he smiled. "Hi ya, Queenie." He gave me his usual grin, and I knew he'd be ok.

"The ring saved her. My mother is going to be okay."

He turned his head and watched as Lucy argued with my mother over the importance of having her heart listened to.

His grin, turned into a much softer smile as he laid his head back on the pillow.

"What happened?" I asked him. "I thought you'd drowned. Ari said that he couldn't find you."

Josh's eyebrows knitted together. "Ari tried looking for me?"

"Yes. He jumped in right after you went overboard. He tried to save you, but you'd disappeared."

Josh looked surprised at this. "I thought you'd be happy to see the last of me, to be honest."

I heard his words and immediately felt bad. I must have treated him pretty poorly if he felt that way.

"When Acania flew over her island before helping Ari, I realized that she was just like me," Josh explained. "She isn't magic herself, but she can channel it through an object. Unlike me, she can store it. That's why she glowed when she saved Ari's life. It was the magic. I knew there had to be something on the island that gave it to her, so when she wasn't looking, I climbed over the rocks and searched the island. I might not be magic, but I know it. I found this ring pretty quickly. It was held to the land by concrete. Most people wouldn't be able to move it, but for someone who can work magic through objects, it was easy enough to touch it and use its own magic against it. It slid through the concrete like butter."

I thought back to when they both went overboard. Just before that big wave knocked them over, Josh was showing something hidden under his coat to Acania. It must have been the ring.

"So how did you get back?"

Josh's face lit up. However he'd managed it, he was sure proud of himself.

"I used the ring. Its magic is based in water, so casting a breathing spell was pretty easy. The ring itself is heavy, which meant I dropped quickly towards the ocean floor, but once I figured out the right spell, I let it use magic to propel me through the water. As soon as I hit land, I came straight here. The ring will recharge itself, and we can use it to help your friends in Havfrue."

A thought suddenly struck me. "What happened to Acania? She went overboard with you."

Josh's expression immediately changed. "Ah. Well, the thing is, she wasn't too pleased to see that I'd stolen the ring. Without it, the sirens can't mask their true selves. They have no magic without it. Your sea witch must have found some other way to channel magic. There are plenty of magical objects under the sea if you look for them. "

"I can imagine." She would be furious no doubt. "What exactly happened to her?"

Josh shrugged his shoulders. "I don't know. Once we'd gone over, I didn't see her. Perhaps she drowned."

Acania drowning would certainly solve all our problems, but she had both wings and a tail and had no problem breathing both in and out of the water. No, she was still alive. There was no doubt in my mind that she was fit and well out there somewhere, and when she realized we'd brought the ring back here, she'd come and find us. Whether she'd be able to hurt us without the ring, I didn't know, but I didn't want to chance it.

I headed to the infirmary door. The disgruntled guard who'd fought with Josh earlier was still there. He bowed when he saw me.

"Can you fetch John to see me, please? Tell him it's very important."

John was by my side within five minutes. It was almost as if he'd been waiting for me to call him.

"Your Highness, how is..."

"Mother is fine. Her illness has passed." I assured him. His eyes opened wide as he took the information in and I knew then he was expecting me to tell him she was dead. That's why he'd gotten to me so quickly. "Lucy is taking very good care of her. It is another matter I need your help with."

The relief on his face was obvious. He and my mother got on well. She was more than his boss, she was his friend too. "I'm so very glad to hear about the queen. I'm afraid I feared the worst. How can I be of assistance to you?"

"Later on, I'll be going out to see Ari. I think I'll be fine, but there is a slight possibility that a group of...of sirens might turn up on our beaches.

John raised an eyebrow. I knew what he was thinking. No one believed in sirens. Not that anyone had believed in merpeople before I started dating Ari.

"They are strange creatures. They are humanoid although some have wings and most have tails. Some have legs. They steal body parts like the sea witch did. Their skin is mottled and mossy. They are hard to describe, but you'll know one when you see one."

John scrunched up his nose in distaste. "What would you like me to do when I spot one, Your Highness?"

"I don't want you personally to go looking for one."

I heard the sigh of relief escape his lips.

"I want you to send our guards out to the shore. As many as you think we can spare. If they spot the sirens tell them to capture them."

"I'm on it," He nodded his head briskly "And once again, I'm so very glad to hear that your mother is well. Please pass on my regards."

I gave him a smile and said I would. I was just about to head back into the Infirmary when I heard a shrill ear-piercing scream come from the infirmary

The Mermaid's Tail

Both John and I ran through the door at breakneck speed. Inside I found Lucy finishing up her exam on my mother with everyone else staring at them. As I got closer, it became apparent why.

The magic from the sea witch had been taken from her in its entirety. Where her legs had been, there was now a tail. She had turned back into the mermaid she once was. Judging by the expression on her face, she wasn't entirely pleased with it. Josh had already jumped out of bed and was trying to prise the ring from Clement's hand, and Anthony was just standing there, shell-shocked at our mother's tail.

"Do something!" she yelled to a rattled-looking Josh.

"I'm trying!" he replied through gritted teeth, but it was apparent that Clement was not going to let him.

"You might be a famous TV star, but that does not mean you know about magic!" Clement yelled, pulling the large iron ring toward him. "This has great power and is not to be used by people who do not know what they are doing."

"I know it has great power, you idiot," retorted Josh. "Why do you think I brought it here? For a fun light show? I brought it to take the spell off the queen. And for your information, I'm from Schnee. You know, the place where everyone is magic? I know exactly what I'm doing."

Both men glared at each other, but it was Anthony who pulled them apart. He tried to take the ring from them, but it burned the tip of his fingers, so it was Clement that ended up with the artifact.

"Gentlemen, please!" I rubbed my temples, trying to decide what to do next. I had my mother who was now perfectly well beyond her obvious distress in gaining her tail back, the people of Havfrue who were still sick to my knowledge and the very real threat of the Sirens coming to get their magic ring back.

I glanced around at everyone. They all stood silently looking at me. Perhaps I'd sounded a tad forceful when I'd last spoken. I decided to go through each problem one by one.

"Mother, you were literally on death's door. I know you don't want a tail, but as you can see, there is magic out there. Once I've taken the ring to Havfrue and saved the people there, I'm sure Josh can whip up a spell to get you your legs back. Until then, try to relax. I promise I won't let the press get a hold of this. Lucy can look after you."

I turned to Clement next. "Clement, thank you so much for your help. Without you, our mother would surely have perished. I will make sure you are handsomely rewarded. Perhaps Anthony can deal with that?"

I glanced towards my brother who nodded his head.

"Finally, Josh. You seem to be the only one who can use the ring. Can you come with Ari and me to Havfrue? There are still a lot of people who need our help."

Josh stood forward, his grin huger than ever. "It would be a pleasure. I'll go and find Seth and meet you down by the rocks!"

I wasn't exactly happy about Josh inviting Seth along to film everything, but I didn't want to hang around to argue. Josh took the ring from Clement's unwilling hand and left with it.

I went through the mental list once again. I thought I had everything covered. It was with a light heart, I walked down to the rocks to meet Ari. Things hadn't turned out exactly as I had expected, but all in all, I'd accomplished everything I'd set out to do. My mother was well...sort of, and I'd soon be able to help all the other people affected by the sea witch. My only real concern was the sirens, but I had John in charge of defense, and I trusted he'd do a good job.

Ari was waiting for me, just as he had said he would be. The top half of his body was out of the water, as he rested his chest on folded arms, his tail splashing lazily behind him. I leaned down to kiss him, but there was a flash nearby that stopped me. Turning, I saw hundreds of people on boats. As the majority of them had cameras, it was easy to guess that they were the media.

"Come under. They can't follow us there." Ari held his hand out to me.

It would have been so easy for me to take it. To slip into the water and escape the media attention, but I'd promised I'd meet Josh here. Without him, we wouldn't be able to save the people of Havfrue.

"Josh saved my mother. He now knows the magic to do it. I told him to meet me here."

Ari looked surprised. "He survived the storm?"

I nodded. "It's a long story. We can't leave without him."

I searched the rocks and the promenade for signs of him and Seth. It was hard to spot anyone in the huge crowds that lined the seafront and, in the distance, the beach. The sea itself was just as crowded. As well as the boats owned or borrowed by the media, I could see some of The Trifork Navy ships that had finally come back to port. John must have sent them back out to keep guard against the sirens.

"What are the media out for?"

I shook my head. It could be one of a hundred reasons. They were sneaky and always seemed to be one step ahead. "They probably saw the naval ships and decided to be nosy."

My toe tapped impatiently upon the rock as we waited for Josh. There was no point going without him as he was the only one who knew how to break the spell. A full ten minutes later, I saw him running along the public promenade, the ring in his hand and Seth following along behind with his camera on his shoulder. Behind him, a group of people chased the pair of them. All had cameras and were snapping away. I guessed that the people in the media didn't really know what was going on, but with a queen, a merman, a celebrity adventurer, and the Trifork Navy involved, they knew there was a story there. I only hoped they wouldn't find out about my mother. I didn't care so much if it the rest of it became public knowledge, but she would be devastated if anyone saw her with a tail.

The palace guards stopped him at the gate that separated the public promenade from the palace's private one. He pointed to me as I waved my arms to signal that it was ok for him to be let in. The people from the newspapers and TV stations carried on filming and snapping their pictures as Josh and Seth navigated the rocks toward us.

"I can't come with you!" Seth wheezed as he reached us just behind Josh. "The camera isn't waterproof."

I heaved a sigh of relief. I had planned to tell them both that Seth couldn't come anyway. My grandfather was extremely shy when it came to the media. He was happy to wave at them above the water, but he was fiercely protective of Havfrue and would never allow anyone from the media down there. I was just about to say such a thing when Josh shouted, "Nonsense," and pushed poor Seth in, camera and all. Instead of the big splash I expected, he floated on the top of the water in a large bubble. I don't know who was more surprised, him or me! Josh leapt out, right through the skin of the bubble to join Seth and before I could object, the bubble sank below the surface.

"I guess that explains how Josh survived underwater for so long," pointed out Ari. Without taking my shoes off, I dived into the water. Ari grabbed hold of my hand so I could breathe, and the four of us made the journey to Havfrue.

The surface of the water was dark thanks to the many boats above us. I asked Ari to pull us deeper so they couldn't film us. My grandfather was going to be livid when he saw Seth and his camera. I didn't want to add to it by letting the media follow us too.

As we swam up to the huge underwater city, I had a premonition that something bad was going to happen.

What if we are too late?

Ari knew what I meant. My mother had been so close to death when we came back, and my grandfather was a much older man.

Ari stopped a passerby and spoke to her. He used the strange underwater language I didn't understand, but once he'd spoken, he translated for my benefit. He spoke to me the way he always did underwater, from his mind to mine.

I asked her how the king is.

The mermaid, an older woman with deep purple hair that was greying at the temples, replied. I didn't need Ari to translate for me to know it was bad news. The mermaid shook as she spoke and had an expression of great sorrow on her face.

However, when Ari did speak to me, the news was not as bad as I feared.

"The king is still alive. He is very sick as are a number of people from Havfrue."

My heart leapt with this information. As long as he was alive, Josh could save him. Ari took off in the direction of the palace at full speed, pulling me along with him. Behind us, I could see Josh and Seth speeding along in their bubble propelled by magic. Josh was full of excitement, gazing around him at this underwater city, but Seth looked like he was just about to throw up. The poor guy wasn't enjoying the ride one bit although I noticed he still managed to keep his camera steady.

The underwater city felt like home in a way that Trifork never really had. The huge irregular buildings, alive with various water plants that swayed in the gentle current and the thousands of tiny fish that darted in and out of the windows enveloped me in a sense of calmness, and brought a joy to my heart. We still had to save my grandfather, but we were so close. I could see the towering palace up ahead, with the top of the strange spire only twenty feet or so below the water's surface. As we swam up the main "road" toward the palace, I noticed something I'd not seen before. Dark shapes behind the palace dotted the landscape or seascape in this case.

No one else had noticed them, but as I watched, they moved. They were getting bigger. At first, I thought they might be some kind of school of fish, but as they came closer, and as their shapes became more defined, it was with terror that I realized what they were.

I'd been so diligent asking John to bring the army to guard Trifork from the sirens that it hadn't occurred to me that they would come to Havfrue first.

And yet they had. Judging by the numbers, Acania had brought her entire tribe, and they didn't look happy. They held makeshift weapons crafted from parts of sunken boats and judging by the expressions on their faces, they weren't afraid to use them.

Havfrue

Ari had seen them now. He didn't say anything. He didn't need to. I could feel it in the way his hand gripped mine just that little bit tighter. We stayed still, the four of us as the sirens swam past the palace.

Acania was at the front. When she saw us, she halted. The few merfolk that had been out and about darted into their homes or into the first window they saw.

She swam right up to me. "I did not expect to find you here. I'm surprised you are not safely back at home in your own palace on land where I'm guessing you have many people assigned to guard you."

I could hear her. Not in my mind, I could actually hear her voice under the water. I couldn't answer her. As soon as I opened my mouth to speak, saltwater flooded into it causing anything I tried to say sound like the strangled gargle it was. Ari had to answer her for me although it was clear it was me she was addressing.

"Her grandfather is sick. We already told you that. We are here to take your friend's spell away from him as well as all the others that she infected."

Acania stared right at me with her one good eye, and I held her gaze. "Ursula was no friend of mine," she said. "And I already told you that. I do not wish to fight you, but you stole something from me. You stole something very important indeed." Her eyes flicked over to the bubble beside us. The bubble that held Josh, Seth, and the large iron ring right at the center.

We'll give it back once we've saved my grandfather and the others. Then you can go home. No one has to get hurt. I said it in my mind to Ari, hoping he could tell her, but somehow she already knew. Maybe telepathy was one of her abilities.

"You have done nothing but lie to me!" She swam right up to me now, her face twisted in anger. It was difficult not to show revulsion at her mangled face and the eye that hung from the socket in the most grotesque fashion. "You stole the ring, you told me that you'd make a video which I'm sure you never intended to make, and unless I'm very much mistaken, aren't those naval ships up there on the surface. Naval ships and boats full of photographers. One lot to kill us, and the other to film it...the killing of the ugly sirens who dared invade your kingdom. You planned it all, didn't you? Not only would you wipe us out, you'd become a hero in the process and still get to keep the ring for yourself."

It's not like that, I protested. *The photographers up there have nothing to do with me. I only want to save my family and my friends from Ursula's spell.*

There was a swish of water in front of my face, and she was gone. When the water cleared a second later, I saw her standing in front of the bubble. Josh held onto the ring tightly as Seth cowered behind him, his camera still rolling, pointing directly at Acania.

She held out her hand, and the ring began to glow red in a similar way to how it had done in the infirmary at the palace. I could see Josh struggling to hold onto it, and as he let go, the ring flew towards Acania at the same time the bubble popped.

They can't breathe!

Ari raced over to them with me in tow. He grabbed Josh but had no hands left to get Seth as well, so I had to grab him. Unfortunately, the magic Ari possessed that allowed whoever

269

he held hands with to breathe worked for me, but not through me. Seth was drowning.

Hold on! Ari said and swam so quickly to the surface that we actually flew into the air before splashing back down.

"I'll have to leave you here," he said as we bobbed around on the surface. "I'll come back when I've dealt with the sirens."

Before I had a chance to stop him, he'd already dived back under the water.

I took a deep breath, and tried to follow. Without his help, I knew I wouldn't get far, but I needed to see what was going on. A hundred feet below me, the merfolk had seen the sirens and those that dared were coming out of their houses to fight. As I watched, the merfolk banded together to form a wall, but although there were many more of them than the sirens, it wasn't a fair fight. The sirens had both magic and weapons.

My lungs began to strain with lack of air, so I had to swim back to the surface.

"What's happening?" Josh asked.

I told him that they were set to fight. He nodded his head and then at the top of his voice, yelled to the nearest boat.

As soon as Seth saw what he was doing, he too began to yell and wave his hands.

"No!" I tried to stop them, but it was already too late. A number of the private boats filled with people from the media were already on their way, as was one of my ships.

"What did you do that for?" I hissed, in a panicked state.

"Your ships have cannons and guns. They will be able to kill the sirens with no problem and rescue us to boot. Are you capturing this Seth?"

Seth held up his camera which was waterlogged. "Nope."

Ignoring Seth, I shouted at Josh. "If they point their cannons downwards, they'll destroy Havfrue and everyone in it. This is Ari's home. My grandfather lives down there as do my aunts. If the Trifork Navy gets involved, they'll wipe out Havfrue completely."

"Oh...I didn't think of that."

Anger coursed through me, but it had nowhere to go. Josh hadn't done it on purpose, he was just an idiot. All I could do was wait for the ship and tell them to retreat. The smaller boats got to us first, and it was with glee that they filmed us and took photos before helping us on board. So much for keeping all of this low key.

I ignored the men on the boat, who were beyond excited to have their queen aboard and kept trying to ask me questions. All I could think of was Ari and what was happening directly below us. I bent over the side, trying to get a good view of everything that was happening below, but I couldn't see a thing, just the rippling of the surface water. If you didn't already know about Havfrue, you'd never know it was there. It was only when the boat began to sway from side to side that I noticed the huge naval ship getting close. The smaller boats were fine bobbing about above Havfrue, but the bulk of the naval ship went deep into the water. It was already too late as I realized that the base of the ship would hit the spire of my grandfather's palace. I didn't see it, but I heard the crash as the ship hit.

I had never felt so utterly hopeless as I did right then. There was nothing I could do to help, and if anything, my being up here was making matters worse. I couldn't even begin to imagine the scene below me, the war between the sirens and the merfolk, and the decimation of my grandfather's palace. I tried to work out just how much of the spire the boat would have hit. With any luck, just the top would have been shattered, leaving the main part of the building intact. No one lived in that grand room. It was my grandfather's throne room. As he was already ill, I doubted he'd be in there, but the not knowing was driving me crazy.

"Sail alongside the ship!" I commanded the one person that didn't have a camera pointing at me. He gave me a quick salute and moved the little boat up next to the ship. A rope ladder was dropped over the side, and when I looked up, I saw Captain Howell peering down at me. I'd not recognized it, but this was the ship we'd all traveled on before.

As I climbed the ladder, I still had no idea what I could do to help those below, but with Captain Howell's help, maybe I could drive the media boats away. Things were bad enough without it all being filmed so that everyone in Trifork could watch it on their TV. Captain Howell held her hand out and helped me onto the ship.

"Your Highness, you can't stay on here long. We hit a submerged rock and are taking on water. I've put out a distress call."

As I looked out towards the shore, I saw that all the boats in the vicinity were now heading toward us—the exact opposite of what I'd intended. When the ship had hit the palace, my only thought had been for the people below. It just hadn't occurred to me that it would damage the ship too. If it was taking on water, it would eventually sink. A ship this size would probably destroy the delicate coral palace completely, as if things couldn't get any worse.

"This is what I want you to do," I said, trying to keep my tone even, although my heart hammered in my chest and my anxiety was at an all-time peak. "Get everybody off this ship quickly. I don't want anyone drowning. If you can get everyone onto another one of the naval fleet, all the better. If you can, try and get the word out amongst my ships to drive the media back. There is a war going on beneath the surface, and I don't want anyone up here accidentally making it worse."

I realized I could hardly say anything about that as everything I'd done up to this point had made everything much worse, but now I had a plan.

"I don't want any ships or boats in this part of the water at all, and I especially don't want any cannon fire or gunshot. Can you do that Captain?"

She raised her hand in a salute and nodded her head.

"What about you, Your Highness? What do you plan on doing?"

"I'm going to save some lives!" I replied, before diving over the side into the ocean. I surfaced quickly and swam to the small media boat with Josh and Seth aboard.

Josh watched me eagerly as Seth resumed filming, this time with someone else's camera.

"Take me to the palace!" I demanded. "Now!"

The captain of the boat turned it around quickly, and we pelted full sail back to the dock by the palace.

Behind me, I heard the first shot of a cannon. Either Captain Howell hadn't passed the message on, or she hadn't been able to.

"Forget the dock," I screamed. "Sail right up to the palace."

The captain of the little boat appeared concerned as he navigated the rocks, but everyone else aboard filmed the action with glee, knowing that this would make the front cover of every newspaper in all the nine kingdoms and dominate the TV news. When the captain was as close as he could get, I clambered overboard, once again, having to swim to make the short distance to the rocks. My destination was to the only person I knew that could help me now. Unfortunately, my way to her was blocked by John and Anthony as I ran through the castle.

"The sirens?" John asked.

I nodded my head as Anthony behind him rolled his eyes at me.

Ignoring him, I explained what was happening. "The ships need to be called off! They are destroying Havfrue."

"I'm on it!" Anthony said, striding off toward John's office which is where he spent most of his time these days.

"He blames me for all this, doesn't he?" I asked, picking up my pace toward the infirmary. John walked alongside.

"He's become very frustrated about how the kingdom is being run. He's grateful that you saved your mother's life, but he thinks someone other than you should have gone to sea. While all this is going on here, he has been keeping on top of the problems at the border."

The trade problems—I'd completely forgotten about them. I didn't even know what the actual problem was. I'd been too busy trying to save everyone. I'd completely forgotten my own job.

"I have one more job for you, and then can you go and help Anthony?"

"Of course, ma'am. However, I can be of assistance."

Of course, my mother looked absolutely petrified when I told her what I wanted her to do.

"I can't! I simply can't!"

I couldn't blame her. I'd asked her to take me out to Havfrue. As a full mermaid, she'd be able to hold my hand so I could breathe underwater. Unfortunately, she'd had a massive phobia about water ever since the sea witch had tried to take me over eighteen years ago. The fact that there were many sirens out there now did nothing to help me persuade her.

"You came onboard the ship for Hayden and Astrid's wedding!" I pointed out.

"And look what happened. I fell sick and don't remember most of it. I may be a mermaid, but the sea and I don't get along."

I sucked in a breath between my teeth. I'd not once won an argument with my mother. She was extremely stubborn at the best of times, and as I was asking her to wade into her worst nightmare, this was hardly the best of times.

"I know you have no real affinity for Havfrue anymore, but Grandfather is still there. He is very sick, and if we don't get to him, he will die, as will many others."

"But..."

"You think the sirens will stop at Havfrue? Once they win there, they will come to Trifork. Now that they have their magic ring, they will lure countless people into the sea, and then they will rip their bodies apart. I can't stop them without your help."

I crossed my fingers behind my back, hoping she wouldn't ask me what my plan was. I'd only thought so far as to get my mother to take me out to sea. Beyond that, I really didn't know what I was going to do. What I did know was that I couldn't just sit around in the palace and watch the world around me crumble without at least trying to do something about it.

It was all well and good for Anthony to feel frustrated at me, but he wasn't the one who would soon be ruling the kingdom. It wasn't enough that I was doing something. I also had to be seen to be doing it. I learned that from my father. He didn't hide out in the palace when he was needed. He jumped into action. It was perhaps the only thing I'd learned. When it came to anything else to do with ruling a kingdom, I was hopelessly unprepared.

"You'll be the death of me, child!" She spoke sternly but pushed herself up into a sitting position. "Come on, John. It looks like there is work to do."

John gave a small smile and then picked my mother up right off the bed.

Thankfully, Lucy was out of the room somewhere, because I knew if she'd seen what we were up to, she'd have insisted on my mother staying in bed. The three of us ran down to the rocks. At the very edge, my mother dove from John's arms gracefully as the photographers on the boats dithered between photographing the queen and her mother, who incidentally now had a tail and all the action going on out on the horizon. The large ships were now pulling back. All except the one Hayden and Astrid got married on, which was almost wholly submerged with only the bow peeking out. All around it, the sea was ominously red, although flashes of green lit it up every few seconds. I couldn't begin to think what was going on down there, but whatever it was, it brought fear to every fiber of my being. The red could only be blood. There was so much of it. The green flashes, I had no clue about. It looked like there was an underwater fireworks display going on.

My mother, whom I knew to be completely petrified, held her hand out to me. Even in the worse moment of her life, she still managed to do it with poise and elegance.

"If I'd have known I was going to be photographed by every member of the paparazzi in the kingdom, I'd have put some make-up on and changed out of this dreadful hospital gown."

If I wasn't so utterly terrified, I'd have laughed.

"I won't be able to speak to you underwater," I told her, "but you just need to swim straight toward the sinking boat."

"I spent the first eighteen years of my life there. I know where I'm going."

I took her hand, and the pair of us sank into the water. It felt like another world down here. All the noise and chaos above was left behind as we swam through the calm depths. All that was about to change. The closer we got to Havfrue, the more nervous I felt at what we might find there.

When we did reach the city, what I did see was the last thing I expected.

The Shark

The red water made everything so much more difficult to see, but it was unmistakable that it was blood. There was no way of telling who it belonged to, but it was safe to say it was more than one being. In the distance, I could just about make out the ship. It had sunk as low as it was going to go, getting caught on what was left of the palace. Looking up, I could see that the very top of it was still peeking out above the surface

As I gazed down, trying to take in the damage, I couldn't quite grasp what was going on. Plumes of underwater smoke floated upwards, coming from buildings that had been damaged by the cannonballs. The 'streets' between them were filled with people fighting which I expected to see. What I didn't expect to see was that the sirens and the merfolk were not fighting each other, but had come together to fight a common enemy. The only thing I couldn't see was what that common enemy could be. I searched among the people, hoping to find someone I recognized, but there were so many of them fighting, it was difficult to see who was who.

"What is going on?" my mother asked, her voice sounding strange in the water. I couldn't answer her back. However the merfolk managed it, speaking underwater was not something I knew how to do. Instead, I pointed to the street where the most people had congregated. All of them were looking toward the palace. The sirens had their weapons raised. Hopefully, someone would be able to tell us what was happening. My mother swam us down to the seafloor and spoke in the strange merfolk language to an elderly mermaid. I couldn't understand what the old woman said, but I didn't need to. At that moment, out of a cloud of red swam my grandfather's shark. In its teeth was a dismembered arm. It was hard to tell if it belonged to one of the merfolk or to a siren. I didn't want to know. At least I now knew what was happening.

The ship had knocked the top off the palace, freeing the only occupant of the room. What with everything else going on, I'd completely forgotten about the shark. The last time I'd seen it, it had saved my life by eating the sea witch. My grandfather had complete control over it, but now it was attacking everyone in its path.

When my mother saw the monster, she tried pulling me back away from it as it dove into the crowd, claiming another victim. A green flash lit up the sea. I looked to the source of the light and saw Acania with the ring. Unfortunately for her, I wasn't the only one to spot her. The shark gobbled down its snack and started to swim towards her. Even from this distance, I could see she was tiring with all the magic she was using. The last time I'd seen her pull magic from it, it had knocked her out entirely.

Everyone else was swimming in the opposite direction, desperate to get away. Without thinking, I pulled myself from my mother's grip and swam as fast as I could toward Acania. I made it just before the shark, but as I pulled her away, I realized two things. The first was that if I didn't get her to safety quickly, we'd both be lunch, and the second was that I couldn't breathe with her, the same way I could with the merfolk. I turned back to my mother, but she was lost in the sea of retreating people. I could feel my lungs screaming in pain as they longed to take a breath. Acania's magic ring could probably save us, but she was now unconscious, and I couldn't channel magic.

Just then, it hit me. I had breathed underwater here before without holding anyone's hand. My grandfather had a room filled with air just for me. I pulled Acania toward the palace and away from the shark.

Most of the palace was still standing. It was just the top that had been destroyed by the ship that was still balancing precariously on top of it. As the doors were no longer manned by guards, getting inside was pretty simple. I swam through the twisting tunnels, pulling Acania behind me. When I'd all but given up, I found the room. Diving through the magical skin that kept the water out, I took a deep breath, filling my lungs. Both Acania and I fell to the sandy bed, and the iron ring rolled across the room before coming to a stop in the sand.

Acania's eyes fluttered open as I tried to get my breathing under control.

"You saved me...again. Why?" she pulled herself up into a sitting position on the sand. She looked so frail and tired. Her left wing was broken. She saw me staring at it and pulled it around her with her hands. I'd never seen someone so lost, so without hope. She'd always been damaged, but her frightful appearance had been something to be scared of, not to be pitied.

"I've done you a wrong."

"You aren't the one who stole our magic," she pointed out. "I know I blamed you, but it was your television friend."

I nodded my head slowly. "You are right. I didn't know about that, but I was the one who sent out my kingdom's ships to stop you. I didn't want you to get to Trifork."

"You were protecting your people. I am trying to do the same."

I sat, looking at her without speaking. She needed my people...any people for hers to survive. They were quite literally falling apart, and the magic they had wasn't enough to rebuild them, only to hide their strange appearances. I could understand everything she'd done. As she said, she was protecting her people. I wished there was something I could do, but without knowing any magic of my own, the only thing that came to mind was giving up some of the people of Trifork, and that just wasn't going to happen.

I didn't know what I could do for her.

"I'll take my girls home. Fighting you has come to nothing for both of us. It has only hurt us all."

I bowed my head down to thank her. She was giving up. It made me feel both happy and sad at the same time. Happy that I'd never have to worry about her and her kind ever again, and sad that there was nothing I could give her in return.

"If you help me find my grandfather, he will call off the shark. Now that you are awake, can you cast a bubble spell around me so I can breathe?"

She cast her eyes over to the ring and held her hand out. The ring flew through the air and landed in her hand. I took her other hand, ignoring how bony it felt and waited as she cast her spell.

I'd not been to my grandfather's bedroom before, but we found it fairly quickly. He lay on the bed, his eyes half open as his redheaded daughters sat around him. With a start, I noticed my mother right by the top of the bed. She must have escaped the shark. Outside, I could just about hear the sound of screams, telling me that the shark was still attacking.

"He has to call off the shark!" I shouted, my voice echoing back at me in the air bubble.

It was my mother who spoke. I still wasn't used to the way she sounded underwater, and I had to concentrate hard to understand her. At least, she wasn't speaking in the weird merfolk language. "He knows the shark is attacking, but he is too weak to call it. He's trying." It was then that I noticed the tears in her eyes.

Acania swam through the bubble, leaving me inside and headed straight for my grandfather.

"Let her pass," I shouted out. "She has the magic to cure him."

"No!" My father opened his eyes wide as Acania placed the iron ring by his side.

I pushed through my aunts. "Grandfather. Acania will save you. She saved Ari and Mother. Please don't fight it."

He shook his head slowly and with great effort. When he spoke, his voice was gravelly and quiet. "You don't understand. I asked for a great many things from the sea witch, and she granted me everything. One of the things was the ability to control the most monstrous killing machine in the sea. I think I've finally gotten through to him and now he is still, but if you take the spell from me, he will continue to kill. He will do as he pleases." I barely heard his last words as he rasped them out.

"The shark is in control now, but only as long as my grandfather can hold on," I repeated. "Is there another cage anywhere?"

My grandfather answered between ragged breaths. "There is no cage big enough or strong enough to hold him."

"Can you do anything?" I asked Acania, fighting the rising panic. It was clear that my grandfather wasn't going to hold out much longer.

"The magic of the ring is complex, but it has limits. It is a water magic and cannot conjure up things that aren't already there. I can create the illusion of a cage, but I cannot make a real one."

An illusion was no good. It might hold the shark for a small while, but he'd soon realize that the bars surrounding him didn't really exist. I wracked my brains trying to think of a place that the shark could be taken. Inspiration struck me.

"Grandfather, can you command the shark to follow Ari and me?"

My mother looked like she was about to object, but my grandfather nodded his head.

"Do it!" I said before my mother could stop me. I could feel Ari nearby. He was very close. I jumped out of the bubble and swam with all my might to the palace entrance. When Ari saw me, he clasped my hand, and I could breathe again.

"I thought you might be here. The shark has stopped, and the sirens are throwing their homemade spears at it, but they just bounce off its thick skin."

"I know," I replied. *"Follow me."*

The shark lay on the seabed. Most of the people of Trifork had already left, but the few that had stayed behind were standing with the sirens trying to kill it. The beast didn't move, but watched them through its beady eyes, waiting for the moment it could attack them back.

When it saw Ari and me, it swam toward us. Ari increased his grip of my hand and began to pull me away from it.

Stop swimming. The shark is under the command of my grandfather. I've asked him to make it follow us.

Ari looked at me then back at the shark unconvinced. *Why would you do that?*

The shark swam alongside us quietly and obediently. It was as tame as a puppy dog...for now, at least.

It would take an army to kill it, and we don't have time to gather an army. We don't have a cage, and my grandfather is on the verge of death.

All the more reason to get out of here as quickly as possible, Ari replied, eyeing up the shark warily.

And let more people die? No. I need you to take us to our cave.

It was my favorite place in the whole world. I loved that cave. Only Ari and I knew about it, and we'd spent so many hours swimming in the light of the phosphorescence hidden away from the rest of the world. I hated that it would now become a cage for a shark, and we'd never be able to go there again, but it was a small price to pay for saving the lives of the people of Havfrue.

Ari understood and pulled me quickly away from the city. The shark followed. Once at the cave, I swam inside for the last time through the small tunnel and pulled myself up onto the little beach. The shark really had to squeeze to get its giant body through, and when it did, it almost filled the cave.

"Stay!" I commanded, as though it was a stray dog. The shark looked at me with murder in its eyes, but through my grandfather's fading magic, it was compelled to obey. It wasn't, however, compelled to enjoy it. I quickly jumped back into the water, and with Ari, we swam around the shark's body and back through the tunnel. On his arm, Ari had picked up an interloper.

"Ollie!" I marveled at the little octopus who loved the cave as much as I did. At the entrance to the cave were a number of rocks. All we had to do was fill the entrance of the tunnel with them so the shark couldn't get out. It was a laborious task, especially as Ari couldn't let go of my hand for any long period of time or I would drown.

We were just over halfway through when the unthinkable happened. Something had happened back at the palace because the shark that had remained placid was now chomping angrily at the stones we'd placed there.

In a panic, I let go of Ari's hand and began shoveling the stones much more quickly while holding my breath. Even Ollie helped by picking up the smaller stones and throwing them into the pile, but it wasn't going to be enough. The shark was chomping through the stones quicker than we could put them down. I touched Ari's arm to take a breath, but the panic I felt, knowing that the shark was soon going to be free made it difficult to breathe. If Acania was here, there might be a chance that she could help us with her magic, but she was a couple of miles away with my mother and grandfather in Havfrue.

Two people, one of which couldn't breathe on her own, plus an octopus that was really still a baby were no match for a razor-toothed killing machine who wanted nothing more than to eat us whole.

We should get out of here!

There was nothing left we could do. The shark would be out in minutes. We had to get as far away as possible so as not to become a tasty entree before it started on the rest of the people of Havfrue.

Ari took my hand, but he pulled me upwards rather than out. A few seconds later and we had breached the surface. I didn't recognize where we were at all. I could see the boats in the distance, but the Trifork palace was nowhere in sight. Large steep cliffs to one side told me that we were just a little further down the coast and that the palace was obscured by a jutting out cliff face. Just a little way ahead of us were more rocks like the ones I scrambled over every day to see Ari. These rocks were so much bigger than the ones we'd been piling up under the water. I followed Ari's lead as he rolled one down into the water.

"You push them into the sea. I'll take them from there and roll them down to the cave entrance."

I nodded quickly and clambered out onto the seaweed covered rocks as he disappeared back under the water. Pushing the rocks into the ocean wasn't as easy as Ari made it look. He was much stronger than I, and many of the rocks had lain as they were for centuries. Using other rocks for leverage, I pushed against them with my feet, rolling the biggest rocks I could into the water, one after the other. The muscles in my legs burned with pain as I pushed them to the very limit, knowing if I wasn't quick enough, the shark would escape.

I pushed the last rock in as the sea nearby turned red with blood. I was too late. The shark had escaped.

Sirens Retreating

I raced down to the edge of the sea, my heart beating wildly at what I might find. I'd only just got Ari back, and now I was about to lose him again. The sea was dark and with the red coloration, I couldn't see beneath the surface. Part of me wanted to dive in, but I knew it was madness to think it. All I could do was wait. I tried seeing if I could feel him. I instinctively knew when he was near or when he was hurt, but now I couldn't feel a thing. Ari was gone, and my heart turned to stone. Something popped up out of the water, and for a second, I had a hope I was wrong, and it was Ari, but it was only Ollie. I held out my arm so he could wrap himself around. At least he was safe. I waited for over an hour for Ari to surface, but he didn't. Nor did I see any sign of the shark. When I could wait no longer, I turned and scrabbled over the rocks to the shore. When I reached the small pebbled beach, I realized I did know the place. It had rocky steps cut into it. If I climbed them I could walk over the land to the palace.

"I'm sorry, Ollie. You can't come with me." I'd been sitting with Ollie in a little rock pool, but he wouldn't survive for too long out of the water. "Stay away from Havfrue, and you'll be ok."

I had no idea if he could understand me, but he seemed reluctant to be let back into the ocean. I hated doing it, but he would die if I kept him on land.

My heart was breaking with each step I took across the grassy field at the top of the cliff. I looked out to the sea, seeing the ships and boats filled with people, desperate to know what was happening. They would be selling newspapers for weeks after this.

When I got to the palace grounds, I didn't know what to do with myself. My grandfather was surely dead by now as was Ari. The shark had probably gone back to Havfrue and was more than likely terrorizing everyone in it. Trifork would survive. No one from the land had been injured as far as I was aware. The people would enjoy the scandal, and eventually, it would die down and be forgotten. I'd go on to be queen and lead the kingdom in quite possibly the most haphazard fashion possible. I'd be alone forever.

Unusually, there were no guards by the gate that led into the palace grounds from this side. Anyone could break in easily. Not that I particularly cared at this point. There was so much going on; they were all probably busy doing other things.

The palace itself was equally free of guards. There was no one there at all. It was so quiet I could hear the squeak of my wet feet on the tiled floor. In the main entrance hall, I dithered, not knowing which way to turn. I could have gone up to my bedroom. It was the most sensible option. I was dripping wet and cold and taking a shower and getting dressed would give me something to do. My mind was numb as I climbed the stairs and not even the heat from the shower revived me. I was cold on the inside, my heart shattered into pieces. No shower could save me from that. I dressed in a t-shirt and jeans, not caring what the media would think of me. My mother was still out there along with my aunts. They would barricade the door to the Havfrue Palace, so there was a good chance that they would be safe. That, at least, was some consolation. I headed down to the office that John and Anthony now shared, but they too were missing. The phone on the desk rang, but I didn't pick it up, knowing it would only someone wanting the gossip. I didn't even know what I would tell them.

Instead, I headed out of the back of the palace. The only way I could think of saving my mother would be to get the navy involved. I didn't know how they would do it, but I was sure they would be able to kill the shark somehow. When I stepped out onto the promenade, a hundred or more light bulbs flashed from the gate that separated the palace grounds from the public grounds. I ignored them. Something else had caught my attention. Out on the rocks, at the spot I usually met Ari, there was a large group of people. A lot of them I recognized as palace guards because of their uniforms, but there were others too. So that's where everyone was. Now I knew where they were, but it didn't explain why everyone was out there. I slowly picked my way across the rocks, aware that I was being watched by every news station in the kingdom.

I pushed my way through the guards. At the waterline, Anthony was helping someone out of the water. When I saw who it was, my heart leapt into my throat. Ari's long hair fanned out on the rocks as he was pulled up onto land. Beside him, my mother pushed him up along with Acania. Blood dripped from his arm, and he was unconscious, but I could see he was alive. His chest rose rhythmically with each breath. That was why I hadn't felt him. It was not that he was dead, but that he wasn't conscious.

"I cannot help him," Acania stated. "I cannot fix normal wounds. You need a land medic. One of your people to help him. I think he will be fine though if you get help quickly."

"Someone go and alert Lucy," my mother ordered. One of the guards shot off in the direction of the palace while Anthony, John, and a couple of guards picked Ari up gently and began to carry him to the palace.

"What happened?" I asked, stuck between wanting to know that my mother would be safe in the water and following the others to the infirmary with Ari.

"There is time to tell you everything. Just know that we are all safe here. I am going back to Havfrue now. My people need me, but I will come home later and tell you everything. Go with Ari. He needs you the most."

I nodded and rushed after Ari, my mind whirring. If my mother thought that everyone was safe, that meant the shark was dead, but I didn't know how. As I passed by the photographers again, I noticed Josh and Seth at the very front.

I spoke to one of the guards quietly asking that they be let in and shown to the dining room. Once I figured everything out myself, I'd give them the exclusive. They'd certainly earned it.

When I got to the infirmary, Ari was already tucked up in bed with Lucy fussing around him. The others had been sent away, but Lucy knew that I'd not leave Ari's side, so she didn't bother to ask.

"He's got a nasty cut on his arm. It looks like he's been bitten. Do you know what happened?"

She rolled some fresh white bandage out and began to wrap Ari's arm.

"I think he was bitten by a shark. Why isn't he waking up?"

Lucy paused and looked at me to make sure I was telling her the truth.

"A shark! Goodness. He's done well not to lose his arm then."

I cared about his arm, but I cared about him more. I waited for her to finish bandaging him up before asking her again why he wasn't awake.

"He's got a bit of a bump on his head. Something has hit him. He's breathing normally, and his pulse is fine. There is nothing else I can do. We just have to wait for him to wake up."

I was about to ask her how long it would be when Ari began to moan.

"Ari!" I sat up closer to him as he opened his eyes. When he saw me, he smiled before wincing.

"I'll fetch some pills for the pain," Lucy said, before bustling off to her little room.

"I thought you were dead!" I said, tears dripping down my face and onto his.

He smiled up at me. "You are going to have to try harder if you want to kill me."

I gave him a puzzled look.

"One of the rocks you pushed off hit the shark right in the middle of the head as he was biting my arm. It was heavy and sharp and killed him instantly. You saved my life."

"So why do you think I was trying to kill you?"

Ari laughed. "Because that wasn't the last rock you pushed down. I was in agony thanks to the bite and didn't get out of the way in time. Thankfully, unlike the shark, I didn't get a direct hit to the center of the head. It must have just hit me on the edge. Not enough to kill me but enough to knock me out."

I brought my hand to my mouth knowing how close I'd come to killing him. I bent forward to kiss him, but the movement on his bed made him wince once again.

"How did you get back here? My mother and Acania were with you."

He shook his head. "I don't remember. I only remember the rock hitting me and then waking up here."

"You've had this stuff before," Lucy said, handing Ari a couple of pills and a cup of water to his good hand. "It will knock the pain on the head, but it will probably make you sleep too. Sleep is the best thing for you right now anyway."

"I don't want to sleep," argued Ari, but Lucy gave him such a stern look that he swallowed the pills right down.

I stayed by his side as the pills took effect. After an hour, Lucy suggested I go to bed myself.

"I'll look after him. You can come back in the morning. Hopefully, he'll be feeling better by then."

Deciding not to argue, I left Ari in her care. There was nothing I could do for him anyway, but I wasn't planning on taking her suggestion.

There were too many things to clear up before I could think about sleeping.

Outside, the sky had darkened considerably and the photographers had finally had enough and gone back home or to their studios. I made my way out to the rocks to wait for my mother. The water lapped quietly against the rocks, and the pale moon glistened on the ocean surface. All the boats were now back in the dock, and the only one I could see was the half-sunken one in the distance. I waited half an hour before my mother emerged. This time she was alone.

I had never been so pleased to see her. It was strange to see her so at peace in the water.

"I'd forgotten how good it feels," she said as though reading my thoughts.

"Do you want me to get some guards down here to help you back to the palace?"

"I'm not coming back, Erica."

Her eyes were glassy, not with the water of the ocean, but with tears. Still, she had a determined look about her. I already knew why. She didn't have to tell me. My grandfather was dead.

"You are the queen now?"

She nodded. She'd been a queen ever since she married my father, but on land, she was second to him. In the sea, as the heir to the Havfrue throne, when my grandfather died, she had automatically become its ruler as I had with Trifork.

I felt tears prick my own eyes, but she wiped them away. "Your grandfather was very old and died with his family by his side. He told me he was very proud of you. It was one of the last things he said."

I nodded. It was a small comfort that my mother was able to be at his side in the end.

"When he passed, we knew that you and Ari were still out there. Acania helped me find him. He was lying next to the dead shark. How is he?"

"Lucy thinks he'll be fine. He'll probably have a scar from the shark bite."

"It will make him look more manly," my mother joked, but there was a sadness in her voice.

"Acania cured the sick in Havfrue. We still have some people with injuries because of the shark, but we will have to deal with them ourselves."

So Acania had come through after all. "Where is she?"

My mother gave a wistful smile. "She took her tribe home. She told me she was too old and too tired to fight anymore. I think this past week did something to her. She took her magic ring, but she was broken."

Sadness crept over me. Acania and the other sirens were hardly innocent, but they'd done the right thing in the end at a great personal cost to themselves. My heart went out to them, knowing how miserable their lives would continue to be.

I sat with her silently for hours. No one bothered us. It was such an irony that now we were in exactly the same position, both elevated to queen by the deaths of our fathers. For my mother, it would be much harder. She knew more about ruling a kingdom than I, but I bet she never thought she'd have to.

"You know, I'm sure Adella could run Havfrue if you wanted to come home," I said eventually.

My mother sighed wistfully. "I've run away from my duties for too long. Havfrue needs me right now. Adella and my other sisters will help. We'll rebuild together."

I bent forward and gave her a kiss on the cheek. It was strange to think of my mother as a mermaid living under water, especially as I'd only ever known her as phobic of it, but watching her swim out, her greying red hair fanned out behind her, she seemed much more at home there than she ever did on land. I gave her a wave as she disappeared into the depths.

The End and The Beginning

Back at the palace, I realized how tired I was. I could barely suppress my yawns as I made my way to the dining room.

It was empty except for a guard in the corner.

"Where are Josh and Seth?" I asked.

"The gentlemen ate a fine meal and then left, Your Highness. They asked me to tell you that they would be in touch shortly."

I thanked him, feeling grateful. I was just too tired to deal with anyone else.

My last stop before bed was to see John. A soon as he saw me, he ushered me out of his office.

"You need to sleep. Anything that can be dealt with will wait until tomorrow. Anthony turned in hours ago, and I was just about to do the same."

The whole kingdom was a mess, but he was right. I needed to sleep and tomorrow was another day.

I dragged myself up the stairs and fell into bed fully clothed.

When I awoke the next morning, the palace couldn't have been more different. No longer quiet as it had been yesterday, I could hear the staff back to their duties and the general hustle and bustle the palace usually had. A maid woke me up and let me know that people were in the breakfast room waiting for me.

I jumped out of bed, wondering who it could be. Today was the day that I'd finally have to answer to the media or there would be a whole load of half-truths and assumptions printed. I already knew that this mess would be on the cover of every newspaper.

Pulling a black dress from my wardrobe, I slipped into it and tied my hair back with a black ribbon. The people of Trifork barely knew my grandfather, but after today, I would make sure they did.

On the way down to the breakfast room, I decided to duck into to the infirmary to see Ari, but his bed was empty. Lucy wasn't around either to ask why.

I found him in the breakfast room. The large, round table was filled with food and surrounded with people. It was so busy, there was only one vacant seat left. I slipped into it beside Ari. John, Anthony, Hayden, and Astrid were also there as were Josh and Seth. They all became quiet as I took my seat. As I did, my stomach gurgled. I couldn't remember the last time I'd eaten.

"We have a lot to discuss," John began.

"I'm sure we do," I replied, "But before we do, let's eat. I'm starving!"

There was a round of applause started by Josh. I guess I wasn't the only hungry one.

I filled my plate with the wonderful pastries and fruit that had been laid out for us and began to eat.

John wasn't wrong when he said there was much to discuss. I planned to send as much aid as we could to Havfrue. We'd saved some of the people thanks to Acania and her magic ring, but others had died because of the shark. It was no real victory, and the people of Havfrue would have to grieve. They would also have to rebuild thanks to the damage caused by my ships.

"I'll be talking to the media today," I said, once most of the food was eaten. "Josh and Seth. Would you like to film it?"

"It would be an honor, Your Highness," Josh said, giving me a wink. He must have felt the weight of the situation. He never called me Your Highness.

"John, would you help me write a statement? The public will already know about my mother. I think it's time that we told them everything. If you didn't already know, she has decided to stay down there and rule alongside her sisters as queen."

"We knew about your grandfather, but we didn't think your mother would want to take up the mantle of ruler," remarked Astrid.

"I was quite surprised myself, but I know she'll do a great job. I'm going to offer her all the support Trifork has to give. Any compatible building materials and medical items will be shipped out to them today."

Astrid gave me a smile which made me feel sad. She was one of the people I'd let down the most.

"I can't let you have another naval ship," I said to her. "As you know we are one short, and we need all the help we can get, but when the madness of today is over, I plan on going down to the dock and purchasing one of the nicest yachts there. My father left me enough money in his will, and I know he would have approved of me doing this. The yacht will be my wedding gift to you. I'll make sure that there is a full crew to take you wherever you want to go and this time...this time I promise I'll not be on board when you go."

Astrid jumped out of her seat and hugged me from behind. "You can come out with us whenever you like."

"Maybe not the first trip, eh?" added Hayden laughing. "You know, everything that has happened does put you in a weird position."

"How so?"

"You are the heir to the throne of Havfrue as well as being the queen of Trifork. When your mother dies...hopefully many, many years in the future, you will have to rule both kingdoms at the same time."

"That reminds me," interrupted John. "While all this was going on, the construction work on the Minster was finished. You can have your coronation at any time. I think under the current circumstances, the faster we do it, the better."

I cleared my throat, knowing what I was about to say would shock everyone. It was the hardest thing I'd ever have to do in my life, and yet I was sure it was the best for everyone.

"There's not going to be a coronation." I waited for everyone to say something, but they all just stared at me open-mouthed. "Not for me, at least. Anthony, you have done an amazing job while I've been away. You know what you are doing more than I, and you seem to enjoy it. There is nothing about leading a kingdom that suits me. I hate giving speeches, I hate the media, and I don't know the first thing about the problems with trade over the borders. I know you could tell me, but I think you could deal with it better than I ever could. Anthony. If you want it, the kingdom, the palace...it's all yours."

There was silence around the table. I could see Josh nudging Seth to film this particular speech, but it was Anthony's reaction I was interested in. A year ago, he wouldn't have been able to do this. Even as recently as a few months ago, I wouldn't have seen him as king material, but since our father's death, he'd shone. He would make a better monarch than I ever could.

"I'm only sixteen," he pointed out, the expression on his face priceless. I could see the excitement through the shock of my announcement. It made me happy that he obviously wanted this as much as I did.

"I know, but you will be seventeen in a couple of weeks. I will serve as the unofficial monarch until your eighteenth birthday next year, but the public will know that it will be you leading the kingdom. I'm sure John will help you."

"I'd be delighted," John answered.

I turned to Josh and Seth. "Don't worry about getting your camera out now. I'll give you a full interview after breakfast. I'll tell you everything."

"What will you do if you are no longer queen?" Josh asked.

I'd been thinking about it for a while. I turned to Ari and gripped his hand.

"Once I've done what I can to aid the people of Havfrue, I'm going back out to sea. Acania told me that the men of her tribe were wiped out. That doesn't mean that there aren't more male sirens out there. I owe her. She saved a lot of people, people that I love. She and her tribe left with nothing. I'm going to find the male sirens."

Josh's eyes popped out of his head with excitement. "Don't dare tell me that I'm not invited on this trip!"

I laughed. "I wouldn't dream of going without you. Maybe I'll become a famous adventurer like you."

"If I let you have any airtime, Queenie. Don't try stealing my thunder now."

Everyone around the table laughed. I gripped Ari's hand tighter and leaned into him, whispering into his ear.

"Say you'll come with me?"

He turned and gazed at me with those beautiful green eyes of his. "I wouldn't miss it for the world."

The End

36230731R00188

Made in the USA
Columbia, SC
23 November 2018